Born in Paris in 1968, **Jérôme Ferrari** is an author and translator who has taught in Algeria, Corsica, and Abu Dhabi. His
2012 novel, *The Sermon on the Fall of Rome* (MacLehose,
2016), won the Goncourt Prize. He is also the author of *Where
I Left My Soul* (MacLehose, 2012), and *The Principle* (Europa,
2017).

Alison Anderson's translations for Europa Editions include
novels by Sélim Nassib, Amélie Nothomb, and Eric-
Emmanuel Schmitt. She is the translator of Muriel Barbery's
The Elegance of the Hedgehog.

ALSO BY

JÉRÔME FERRARI

The Principle

IN HIS OWN IMAGE

Jérôme Ferrari

IN HIS OWN IMAGE

*Translated from the French
by Alison Anderson*

Europa
editions

Europa Editions
1 Penn Plaza, Suite 6282
New York, N.Y. 10019
www.europaeditions.com
info@europaeditions.com

Copyright © 2018 by Actes Sud
Published by a special arrangement with Actes Sud in conjunction
with their duly appointed agent 2 Seas Literary Agency
First Publication 2022 by Europa Editions

Translation by Alison Anderson
Original title: *À son image*
Translation copyright © 2022 by Europa Editions

Library of Congress Cataloging in Publication Data is available
ISBN 978-1-60945-670-4

Ferrari, Jérôme
In His Own Image

Book design by Emanuele Ragnisco
www.mekkanografici.com

Cover photo © Greta Lorimer

Prepress by Grafica Punto Print – Rome

Printed in Italy

CONTENTS

In mimoria di u me cucinu caru, Jean Vesperini

Thou shalt not make unto thee any graven image,
or any likeness of any thing that is in heaven above, or that is in the
earth beneath, or that is in the water under the earth.
Thou shalt not bow down thyself to them, nor serve them.
—EXODUS 20:4–5

Obscene! She wanted to cry but did not cry because she did not
know at whom the word should be flung: at herself, at West, at the com-
mittee of angels that watches impassively over all the passes. Obscene
because such things ought not to take place, and then obscene again
because having taken place they ought not to be brought into the light
but covered up and hidden forever in the bowels of the earth [. . .].
—J. M. COETZEE
Elizabeth Costello

Death has passed by. The photograph comes afterwards
and, unlike painting, it does not suspend time but fixes it.
—MATHIEU RIBOULET
Les Oeuvres de miséricorde [Merciful Acts]

PRAYERS AT THE FOOT OF THE ALTAR

1
(On the Way Home, Vojvodina, 1992)

The last time she saw him, ten years earlier, he was on his way home, and she was accompanying him. He hadn't said a word from the time the bus from Belgrade had dropped them off at the bus station. And then he'd paused, still silent, to lean against the railing of a bridge over the Danube that the NATO bombings of 1999 would soon reduce to only rubble and towers. Antonia stood a few steps behind him, observing him, her camera in her hand. He was wearing torn military fatigues on which he'd sewn his sergeant's stripes, and beneath the insignia of the now-dissolved JNA[1] was the Serbian coat of arms with its two-headed eagle surrounded by four firesteels. At his feet lay a big duffel bag containing only a Hungarian edition of Imre Kertész's *Kaddish for an Unborn Child*, the first volume of a Serbo-Croatian translation of the complete works of Bukowski, and a few cassettes of R.E.M. and Nirvana; he could not even remember the last time he had listened to them. He was holding his head in his hands. He wasn't looking at the dark waters of the river, or the sky heavy with rain. A group of adolescent boys slowed their pace as they passed close to him on the bridge, and they burst out laughing, an incomprehensible laugh, blatantly looking him up and down. Antonia took the shot, the last of the feature she was devoting to him, that would never be published. At first he did

[1] Yugoslav People's Army

not seem to react. Then he looked up, and Antonia saw he was weeping. He picked up his bag, but as she prepared to follow him, he waved his hand to stop her, and she stayed on the bridge watching him walk away until he had disappeared and it was too late for any other form of farewell.

Now on this Friday evening in August 2003, in the port in Calvi, she recognized him immediately. Dragan was walking toward her among the crowd of tourists with another NCO from the Foreign Legion, and this time his uniform was impeccable. She stopped. When their eyes met, he smiled, and went up to kiss her with a warmth that was absolutely genuine. She was so moved that at first she did not realize he was speaking to her in French. He pointed to the camera slung across her shoulder. Are there interesting things to take pictures of around here? She burst out laughing. No. Really nothing interesting. She took wedding photos now, and that was why she was in Calvi. Pictures of wedding rings. Emotional families. Couples, obviously, lots of couples, posing in front of flower beds, luxury cars, or the sun dipping into the Mediterranean. Always the same things, oddly grotesque, repetitive, and ephemeral all at the same time. She earned a decent living, but it certainly wasn't interesting. She fell silent. She was afraid he might be able to sense how bitter she had become. She asked him if he'd like to go for a drink. He was on call. Had to get back to camp at Raffalli. But he'd be glad to spend tomorrow evening with her. Antonia had planned to go home, in the south of the island, once the wedding was over. She had promised her parents she'd have dinner with them. He shrugged. Couldn't she stay one more day? She looked at him. Of course she could.

She called her mother to tell her that something had come up obliging her to stay in Balagne a day longer. She wouldn't be able to have dinner in the village Saturday evening as promised, but she'd be there for sure the following day. Even though Antonia tried to make the sudden change of plans seem as innocuous as possible, it nevertheless almost immediately triggered a tearful indictment where she was reproached for her casual, selfish, ungrateful attitude. Antonia did not make the mistake of getting angry. She assured her mother of the perfection of her daughterly love, told her she was looking forward to seeing her on Sunday, and reduced her to silence by more or less hanging up on her. Then she switched off her cell phone and went to bed.

All day long she tried to focus on her work. She photographed the young bride from the moment she left her bathroom until she put on her gown, unanimously deemed sublime by her swooning entourage; she photographed the inevitable radiance of the groom's smile the moment he saw his betrothed; she followed them to the church, took pictures during the banquet of all the guests dazed with heat and alcohol, and ended the day on the beach, where she granted herself the guilty pleasure of having the newlyweds pose at length beneath a scorching sun in sophisticated poses she hoped were as painful as they were ridiculous. By the end of the session they had worked up a sweat but were thrilled. They were sure the results would be magnificent, just as the day had been. They paid Antonia, thanking her profusely, and she was able to go and join Dragan for dinner. They talked all night, and when she got back to the hotel, it was five o'clock in the morning. She wasn't sleepy. If she went to bed and managed to fall asleep in spite of everything, she would still have to vacate the room at eleven. She decided to set off right away. She would stop off at her place, sleep all day, and then go up to the village for dinner with her parents. She sat at the wheel and rolled down all the windows. It was still dark out, and the temperature had not gone below eighty-five. She went through L'Île-Rousse. On the Ostriconi road as she came around a bend, although the sea below her still lay in the shadow of night, the sun, its glow vaguely coloring the sky behind the mountains, suddenly rose above the peaks, and its first rays lit up Antonia's face. She let herself be dazzled for a moment, and closed her eyes.

Her parents and her brother, Marc-Aurèle, waited for a long time. They kept getting her voicemail. By nine o'clock that evening, her mother had abandoned indignation for despair once and for all. All three left the village to go down into the town, rang in vain at the door of Antonia's apartment, questioned the neighbors, went down every street in the neighborhood every which way looking for her car until finally they went to the gendarmerie. The following day, late in the afternoon, two gendarmes came to the village, and Antonia's mother began to scream the moment she saw the expression on their faces. They confirmed that what she had been dreading—not just these last twenty-four hours but basically her entire life—had happened. Their colleagues from Balagne had found Antonia's car at the bottom of a ravine near the Ostriconi river. It had taken them some time. It was almost impossible to see it from the road, and there were no skid marks on the asphalt to help them with their search. They'd had to use a helicopter. In all likelihood, Antonia had died the day before, at dawn. The gendarmes wanted to leave, but Antonia's father insisted on offering them coffee; they drank in silence, standing in the kitchen, eyes down and caps in hand.

Two days later, the coffin is placed on a modest catafalque in front of the altar between two tall white candles. The priest coming forward to bless it is Antonia's uncle on her mother's side. The same priest who, thirty-eight years earlier, in that very church, had held her to his chest as the cold water from the baptistery was sprinkled on her forehead, making her cry. At the time he was seventeen years old. He was not interested in the ritual. All he could think of was how to comfort the little child wriggling in his arms.

Now he says, *Then will I go unto the altar of God*, and the congregation responds: *To God who giveth joy to my youth.*

The words of the liturgy are not hard to say. They do not belong to him, they exist without him, they require neither his sorrow nor the untimely tenderness of his memories, merely the material presence of his body in order to become incarnate, alive, through him. It is painful, however, to hear the congregation's response. It is as if all these voices have united to become Antonia's voice, and that she is the one who is speaking, one last time, in a strange, multiple voice, before she will be reduced to silence. For a moment he is afraid he will be carried away by his emotions, irresistible and inappropriate. All he can do is entrust himself to the grace of God.

He says, *Our help is in the name of the Lord.*

He hears the buzz of conversation of people who could not find room inside the church and who have stayed outside to wait for the end of the ceremony to offer their condolences. There are many of them. Premature death is always, and all the more so when it is sudden, an outrage, with a formidable power of seduction. From the altar he can see the crowding in the pews of both villagers and strangers, sees his more or less distant cousins, his brothers and, in the first row, very near the coffin, his sister and brother-in-law, and Marc-Aurèle weeping unrestrainedly. He could have refused to celebrate the mass, could have been standing there beside them. If he had, he too might be weeping. But Antonia has no use for yet more tears. Now he is sure: his place is here, at the foot of the altar, it is here that he is closest to his departed goddaughter, closer than he has been in a very long time.

REQUIEM ÆTERNAM

2

(Family of Tourists Walking Toward the Beach,
South Corsica, 1979)

swimsuits and in color, and the old veiled women whose inevitably glum expressions were proof that this world here below was indeed the vale of tears evoked in the Psalms. Antonia's godfather initially thought she was interested in her origins, and he offered to guide her along the tangled pathways of her genealogy: women who were widowed too young, who remarried, siblings with different parents, the inevitable unwed mothers, and subtly consanguine unions, all of which contributed to make this family tree dark and confusing to the neophyte. He made a considerable effort, sometimes in vain, to identify unknown individuals and determine their degree of kinship, but Antonia showed no more than polite interest. This was not the enigma that captivated her. She did not seem to care whether she belonged to the family that had left its trace on the glossy paper. The enigma was in the existence of the trace itself: the light reflected by bodies now grown old or long turned to dust had been captured and preserved through a process whose miraculous aspect could not be exhausted by simple technical explanations. Antonia studied a portrait of her mother at the age of ten, standing in front of the house in the shadow of the laurel tree and next to a tiny, ancient relative who, appropriately, was grimacing for all she was worth; then she recognized her godfather, at the same age, among other pupils gathered in the village schoolyard for the class photo, and the house, the schoolyard, even the laurel tree, did not seem to have changed, but the ancient relative was dead, her mother and godfather had not been children for a long time now, and their vanished childhood had nevertheless deposited on the film a trace of its reality as tangible and immediate as a footprint in clay, and to Antonia it seemed that all these famil-iar places, and from these places the immensity of the entire world, were filling with silent forms, as if all the moments of the past were surviving simultaneously, not in eternity, but in an inconceivable permanence of the present. Yet Antonia knew very well that all adults had once been children, she knew that the dead had been alive and that the past, no matter how distant, began as the present; therefore how could proof that such commonplaces are true be enigmatic or deeply moving? It was pointless to try to find an intelligent or profound answer to this question; the photographs opposed any quest for depth with the impenetrability of their surface.

Clearly this new passion of his goddaughter-niece's was anything but a whim. As it happened, he was proven right, but his certainty was in no way a product of wisdom. In truth, his trust in Antonia was blind; everything she did or said seemed admirable to him, and if she did get caught out now and again, he always assumed that deep down it was for some secret, noble reason. Ever since he had carried her to the baptismal font that Sunday morning in the summer of 1965, at a time when his own relationship with God did not exist and he had a terrible hangover after a night spent at one of the bars in town, he had felt an infallible bond with her, a bond of blood and spirit. He loved her as if she had actually become his daughter, through the grace of a sacrament to which, at the time, he did not attach any importance, and this love—until an unexpected and imperious call caused him to collapse on his own road to Damascus—was the only love he could truly feel without restrictions or limits. His sister reproached him for it, predicting that he would turn Antonia into an unbearable spoiled brat, and she did not like the fact that once again he had to stand out by giving her a gift as outrageously lavish as a camera. She liked it even less when Antonia, in the weeks that followed her birthday, far from getting bored with her new toy, began to constantly threaten family members and unwary visitors with her lens. It became necessary to invoke the permanent confiscation of her camera to get her to resign herself to photographing animals, flowers, landscapes, and buildings, all things that yielded with docile indifference to her voracious appetite. Antonia despaired. She was not interested in animals or flowers, only human beings, and now on top of it all she had begun screwing up her pictures. Despite the fact that she kept a scrupulous record in a notebook of all her apertures and shutter speeds, all the images she produced were blurry, too dark, or horribly overexposed. Whenever she went to collect her prints, she came away disheartened. She was making no progress, and it was costing such a fortune that her parents had to agree to let her set up her own darkroom in the cellar. She learned to develop her negatives herself, amid the acid effluvia of developers and the rosé wine her father bought wholesale from the cooperative before bottling it himself. She eventually managed to master her erratic exposure times and focus correctly. But even then she was not satisfied. She had to concede that most of the moments captured hardly deserved to be miraculously torn from their empty transience. Only when the month of August 1979 came along did she, almost inadvertently, take the first picture she judged worthy of keeping.

Pascal B. and his friends invited Antonia, Madeleine, and Laetitia O., along with a few other village girls they had dangerously ceased to regard as children, to go down to the town for ice cream. They parked their cars along the port. The cafés were set out in a row along a street that led to the beach and that had to be crossed to reach the seaside café terrace where Antonia, camera in hand, sat down with the girls. The boys stayed on the other side of the street, sitting at a table out on the sidewalk, except for Pascal B., who was leaning against the wall by the door with a cup of coffee in his hand. He was wearing an outfit that consisted of a white tunic and trousers, with colorful Indian-inspired embroidery, and woven moccasins, also white. He was nineteen back then, and Antonia found him irresistible. She studied the group for a long time through her viewfinder, focused carefully, and waited for a troublesome waiter crossing the street to vanish inside the bar. Just as she pressed the shutter release, some passersby she hadn't seen approaching suddenly appeared from the left in her viewfinder. Tourists, a man and a woman in their forties, with their two children. They were heading toward the beach, barefoot, wearing only their swimming things, their towels thrown over their shoulders, unaware that, through the unforgivably casual gesture of their intrusion, they had ruined Antonia's meticulous composition. But when she developed the print, Antonia discovered to her astonishment that it was perfect—thus learning that she should never despair of the prodigal nature of chance: the print shows the boys all glaring with disapproval and disgust toward the left of the image, where the carefree tourists are striding along beneath the shop sign of the bar. Pascal B. has also turned toward them, but his gaze expresses a great deal more than mere disapproval or disgust. The tourists are going along their way, smiling as if the extraordinarily hostile world around them did not exist. It is impossible to determine whether their blindness is the result of innocence or scorn. The photograph does not show, although it clearly signals the possibility, that only a second later, in turning abruptly to his wife, the man will bump into Pascal B., who will spill his coffee and stare for a split second, stunned and incredulous, at the brown spots now staining his elegant white outfit. The guilty man opened his mouth, perhaps to offer a pointless apology, but Pascal B. did not leave him the time to speak: he gave him a headbutt. The tourist raised his hands to his nose then fell to his knees on the sidewalk. The woman rushed toward him, shouting at Pascal B., who shoved her roughly against the wall. He went over to the man on the ground and kicked him in the ribs, a first time, then again, showering him with insults. The tourist curled up where he lay, trying to protect himself as best he could. In the bar, no one lifted a finger to help him. The terrified children began screaming and crying. The woman, her shoulder and back now grazed and bleeding, took them in her arms, crying, too. Antonia and the girls went closer to have a look. Everyone was looking. Suddenly Pascal B.'s anger subsided. He stood there breathing heavily, his gaze vacant, then he turned on his heels and went into the bar. The man stood up, his face covered in blood, and continued on his way with his wife and children. Antonia heard laughter. Strangely enough, although she complained of the lack of interesting subjects, she hadn't taken more pictures. She knew she had done the right thing: the humiliation of a man who is given a hiding in front of his children, his terror and weakness, and, worse yet, the sordid frisson of collective pleasure felt by all the onlookers—all of that must disappear forever into the abyss of the past. Antonia had not yet encountered the gaze of the Gorgon, but she had sensed its presence for the first time and heard the hissing of the snakes in its hair. Her mouth was dry, and she felt queasy, vaguely ashamed, and also incredibly excited by what she had just witnessed—this outburst of pure violence, so disproportionate that it became totally gratuitous—she had liked being near it, she understood what it meant, and when Pascal B. came out of the bar where he had tried in vain to remove the coffee stains with a damp cloth, she found him even more attractive. In the car on the way home, the other boys congratulated him and slapped him on the shoulder. He stared at the road as he drove, not answering, not smiling. When he dropped her off at her house, Antonia wanted to take a close-up of him at the wheel of his car, but she didn't dare ask him to pose. She sent the picture she was so pleased with to her godfather at the seminary so that he could delight in her progress. In the accompanying letter she did not mention the incident or the disturbing ambivalence of the feelings stirring inside her. She went on sending him those pictures, ever greater in number, that she was pleased with. In February 1981, she gave him a framed enlargement of a shot she had taken during his ordination where he is lying flat on his stomach, overcome with joy and emotion, his heart pounding on the freezing flagstones of the cathedral in Ajaccio.

Now the bell has rung for the first time, and with his purple chasuble and stole over his shoulders he is waiting for the coffin to arrive, trying in vain to pray by the statue of Our Lady of the Rosary. He knows that the experience of abandonment and terrible solitude is intrinsic to faith, but in this moment he does not have the strength to endure it. He is still afraid he will be incapable of celebrating the office for the dead. When two days ago his sister called to ask him to do it—or rather demanded he do it—just after she had informed him of Antonia's death, at first he refused, indignantly, how could you? You know very well that it's not my place, my place is at your side, but she would not listen, and no matter how foolishly, pointlessly, he repeated, it's not my place, listen to me, she kept interrupting, saying, no, you listen to me, if you refuse to do it, they're going to send us a Franciscan, a Belgian, a Mexican, a Laotian, or who knows what, it makes no difference, no one can understand a word they say, they make everyone laugh, even during funerals, you can hear people snorting and laughing hilariously, they don't even realize, they're deaf and senile, they're all senile, they get the names all wrong, can you imagine? they cannot even be bothered to read the plaque on the coffin properly, last month at the funeral of old Jean-Charles P., the priest called him Jean-Simon during the entire mass, no one dared say a thing, it was a disgrace! and besides, they go way overboard, they could keep it to a minimum, say the mass, bless the body, and go back to their monastery, but do you think that's what they do? of course not! they start in on these interminable homilies, you have no idea, there's no end to it, and of course no one understands a thing, how can they possibly imagine for even a second that they know how to speak French? it's unbelievable! and it's just as well no one understands a thing, they don't know us, they know nothing about us, they must be making up any old thing, one cliché after another, a pack of lies, and I don't want some senile Belgian who does not know my daughter to talk to us about her and make everyone laugh by calling her Jeannine or Roberte or God knows what, I don't want him to make us look ridiculous, and tarnish her memory, even with all the best will in the world, and neither do you, you don't want that, you could not possibly want that. You've got to do it, and that's it. Don't tell me it's not your place. Where else are you supposed to be? She was right, of course, the Franciscans really were for-eigners, or senile, or both at the same time, and they spoke some mumbo jumbo full of cheery noises that would only serve to seriously endanger the solemn nature of any ceremony, par-ticularly a funeral. And so he said to her: you're right, and he capitulated. Even if she'd been wrong, his capitulation would have remained, for all that, the only conceivable solution, for his sister expressed herself with implacable pugnacity, in a tone that would not brook the slightest contradiction, although she had not slept for thirty-six hours, and, just last night, with no news from Antonia, who had not returned from Calvi and wasn't answering her phone, she could not finish a sentence without bursting into tears, saying over and over in a broken voice that something awful must have happened, she was sure of it, and it was so exasperating he could not even bring him-self to feel concerned, to imagine for even an instant that it could be true, but it was true and now that this awful some-thing had happened, she was no longer weeping. The entire future, all of a sudden, was reduced to the organization of the funeral. She just had to do her duty and bury her daughter, and she was devoting herself to that single task so thoroughly—eliminating all the obstacles one after the other, her own brother's reluctance for a start, anything that might prevent her from fulfilling her task—that she had no more room inside for sorrow. A sad subterfuge, he thought. My poor sister. He felt infinite pity for her, but he could not help but recognize in that suspicious pity the same pathetic expedient he was using to fend off his own sorrow.

The next day he left his parish and went to Ajaccio. His nephew Marc-Aurèle was waiting at the airport. They embraced, and Marc-Aurèle said, I'm glad you'll be saying the mass, she would've been glad to know it's you, and he began weeping on his shoulder like a little boy. The heat was crushing. He could feel his nephew's breath on his neck, his sweat, his burning tears, and he stepped back as tactfully as possible. Let's get going. They set off beneath a white sky. Marc-Aurèle drove in silence at first. From time to time he sniffled and wiped his nose with the back of his hand, snot leaving gleaming trails on the sleeve of his black suit, and then he began to speak. He got lost in conjectures that were completely devoid of meaning, oh! if only she hadn't gone to Calvi, he was indignant because the bride's family in Balagne had called the house, hastily expressing their condolences then asking if, all the same, would it be possible to have the pictures sent to them—can you imagine? and sniveling he said, she loved photography so much! The priest closed his eyes. He breathed in the scent of the maquis through the open window and forced himself to remain silent. He did not ask Marc-Aurèle: how can you be so completely clueless as to who your own sister was? Then Marc-Aurèle suggested they could place Antonia's camera next to the coffin, during the mass, with a portrait of her, in memory of what she loved, what do you think, that would be nice, wouldn't it?

He turned abruptly to his nephew. He almost shouted: no! No, it's out of the question.

It was strange, really, this unwavering liking of Marc-Aurèle's, ever since he was a child, for the stupidest, commonest ideas. When they happened to be utterly grotesque, like the one he had just ingenuously formulated, there were no limits to his enthusiasm. If you let him, he would screen a slideshow during mass, maybe he'd even want to read a poem, obviously one he himself had written, and he would surely start sobbing as he read it. In one respect, he was far more dangerous than an entire horde of verbose, senile Franciscans. But his sorrow was great, and it deserved a different answer, not a harsh refusal. Marc-Aurèle, my boy, continued the priest in a tone that tried to show compassion, tomorrow won't be about evoking your sister's life, what she liked or didn't like. It won't even be about showing how sad we are. Tomorrow, we commend your sister to God, and we pray that He will receive her. That has nothing to do with cameras and portraits, nothing to do with our personal memories. Do you understand? And Marc-Aurèle nodded in silence, not because he had understood, but because he was docile, a trait the priest could not help but think was worthy of scorn. If God absolutely had to take one of his sister's children, why couldn't He have taken this one? He chastised himself for the horrible sincerity of that thought, but he could not banish it from his mind. He was unfair, and cruel, with no true love. The little love of which he was capable flowed only toward her, this young woman he now had to lay to rest. Anything left over could come only from a supernatural spring which, for the moment, had dried up. His lip trembled, and he held back the tears welling in his eyes. He placed his hand on his nephew's shoulder.

In the village, they worked their way through the crowd that had gathered in the sun in front of the house. As they passed, cheerful discussions ceased for a moment, hands reached out to them, clutched at them, they had trouble getting from one embrace to the next, Marc-Aurèle began crying all over again on a stranger's shoulder, and the priest continued on his own through the baking heat, blinding sweat streaming down his brow while people called out to him from every side,

using his name or shouting, "Father!," he had no time to figure out who they were, those who took him in their arms and
only let him go once they had left burning kisses on his cheeks,
and he eventually made it through the door and into the house
where conversations were going on in the kitchen and the dining room, in low voices, over steaming coffeepots, bottles of
water already lukewarm, and cakes, and the darkened rooms
were no cooler, motes of dust danced in horizontal streams of
summer light that filtered through the blinds onto the rough-
cast white wall, a thermometer the shape of Corsica showed a
hundred degrees, and he entered the room where Antonia lay,
the almost perfect silence troubled only by the buzzing of flies.
People came in, regularly, their steps slow and fearful, as if they
were afraid they might wake a child, they crossed themselves
by the body, stood in thoughtful contemplation for a moment,
then went back out, showing equal care. Sitting by the bed
were his brother-in-law and sister, who greeted each newcomer
with a nod. He went to embrace them. They said nothing. He
looked at Antonia. Her hands were joined over the white
sheet, and on her left eye was a bruise made even more hideous
by some clumsy makeup. A handkerchief had been placed over
her mouth and chin. Perhaps her jaw had been broken in the
accident. Perhaps the funeral home employees had had to
break it themselves because the rigor mortis prevented them
from closing her mouth. The smell of decomposition was
clearly noticeable. Antonia had stayed more than thirty hours
in her car, in the very midst of the heat wave, before she was
found, and there were limits to the art of embalming, particularly when it was practiced by personnel who were clearly
incompetent. Probably the best thing would have been not to
display her in such a state. His sister had not been guided by
any considerations of propriety, and he thought she was right.
One must not flee the sight of death. One must not embellish
it. Even bruised and rotting, even deserted by the soul and

You'll be singing polyphony, I imagine?

They nod.

Do you need me to cue you when to come in?

No, Father. We know the liturgy. We sing a lot of masses.

Well then, that's fine.

But we wanted to ask you, would you like us to sing everything, the *Dies iræ,* the *Libera me,* because some priests don't—

Everything, he said, interrupting the young man. Sing everything you can. And all the couplets of the *Dies iræ.*

One of the singers asks timidly: You don't think it might be a bit long?

He smiles bitterly and replies: A bit long? Long for who?

He motions to them to go and stand by the altar. He goes out onto the square in front of the church. Heat haze is floating on the horizon, above the sea. There are already a lot of people. A few men start to move toward him to present their condolences yet again, but then they think better of it and continue their conversation. At this point, and for the length of the ceremony, he is no longer the dead woman's uncle but simply a priest. He recognizes Simon T., sitting all alone on a wall, his eyes red. Before he was called to the priesthood, he and Simon's mother, Damienne T., a widow ten years his senior, had been living together. It was particularly painful to recall that the first effect of his vocation had been to inflict a wound of irreversible abandonment upon this woman whom he had already made to suffer so greatly by loving her so poorly and so little, as if grace could only be obtained at the exorbitant price of an indelible sin. He goes up to Simon, who stands up, and takes him in his arms. The bell rings for the third time. The hearse pulls up outside the church. Four men take out the coffin and hoist it onto their shoulders. The priest precedes them down the path to the altar.

When he hears the opening strains of the *Requiem*, his doubts vanish instantly. They sing perfectly, not forcing it, with just the right amount of piety, and their voice is that of the congregation, of Antonia, and of Christ still hoping the bitter cup might pass from him, the voice of weakness and hope, and in her chapel, the Virgin of the Rosary seems to have come alive again. She was no doubt the work of some mediocre artist from Lucca or Livorno, a talentless charlatan who had to abandon sculpture to start producing lucrative relics—splinters transformed into fragments of the True Cross, images of the holy Face painted on the grayish cloth of carefully frayed shrouds, tiny fragments of kneecap or thighbone carved from sheep's bones and set in gold—and who threw the statue into the sea in a fit of lucid despair, never thinking it might one day become an object of worship. But it is said that when the fishermen of Campomoro found her stranded on the beach, her rosary in her hand, they were unable to lift her. The news of the miracle spread. Men came down from the mountains all around, but for all the fervor of their votive prayers, not one of them could move the Virgin, who obstinately opposed them with the miraculous mass of her weight. She only consented to lightness for two old men from the village, who set her down in the chapel where her place had been waiting for her since time began. Everyone rejoiced at this paltry sign of favor—the only sign, it's true, that had ever been addressed to them. The priest, of course, never believed the childish miracle could be real. As time went by, human naïveté had no doubt transfigured the random arrival of the statue into a decree from Providence. Clearly, they also seized the opportunity offered to them to satisfy their ancient tendency toward idolatry. It hardly mattered, in the end. As he well knows, there is nothing so humble that it cannot welcome and make manifest divine presence—and that is the true miracle, so much so that at that very moment, when the voices begin to sing the Psalm *Te decet hymnus*, he himself can almost feel the painted wood trembling.

KYRIE ELEISON

3
(Woman Fleeing from a Fire, Alta Rocca, 1983)

way from the hotel to the police station, carrying their unloaded weapons over their shoulder, and Antonia wept before her television as she watched them move slowly forward through the night. Pascal B.'s case, along with that of his comrades, was referred to the State Security Court, and they were placed in custody at the Santé prison. She wrote to him nearly every day. She took pictures for him—his friends waiting for his return, the deserted streets, the arrival of spring—and sent them to him. He asked her not to be alarmed if he didn't answer very often. He didn't like writing, and the monotony of prison life was such that he would not have had much to tell her, but he waited eagerly for her letters and photographs and told her he wasn't sorry for anything he had done but could not wait to see her again and to see everything which, thanks to her, still existed, at least in the form of images he pinned to the walls of his cell. At the end of the summer he was released. A party in his honor was organized in the schoolyard. Everyone rushed up to see him and embrace him. Simon T. followed him everywhere, gazing at him fervently, that gaze ordinary people reserve for demigods, and he turned bright red every time his hero gratified him with a smile and a friendly little pat on the back of his neck. Any attention Pascal B. paid to Antonia was distracted at best, and she was so hurt that she took no pictures at the party, her heart wasn't in it. But at the end of the evening, when she was mournfully getting ready to go home, he pulled her to one side, took her in his arms, and thanked her. I will never forget what you did for me. He caressed her hair and placed a single, chaste kiss on her lips. Then he said, go home now. I'll wait for you. And he actually did wait. He waited two years. One evening in July 1982, he picked Antonia up in his car and drove her outside the village. He parked on a dirt track off the main road. He kissed her far less chastely than the first time, began breathing heavily, and penetrated her on the back seat after he had removed just those clothes that might be an obstacle to his pursuit. When it was over, he pulled up his trousers and went out to smoke a cigarette that glowed red in the darkness. Antonia used her T-shirt to wipe off the sperm smeared on her belly, then she groped about in the dark looking for her underpants and eventually found them under the passenger seat. She went out to join Pascal B., putting her arms around him, tenderly, from behind, her cheek against his shoulder. He turned around and held her close, covering her with kisses. There hadn't been much pain or much pleasure, and no blood at all. It hadn't really been the way she'd imagined for so long, but that was okay. She was having a thrilling adventure, and she felt full of love and gratitude. From that night on, and every night when he did not mysteriously disappear, he took Antonia to the same place at the same time. She would be talking with Madeleine and Laetitia, sitting on the terrace of the village bar, Pascal B. would be with his friends drinking at the bar counter, and then he would come out and motion to her, and she would follow. He didn't talk as he drove, he stared at the road, gravely. As soon as he had stopped the car on the dirt track, he kissed her fiercely, and after that, once Antonia had enough experience and boldness for their relationship to have a definite, established ritual, he would relax back into the seat and stare into the middle distance while she leaned over him, undid his trousers, and sucked him, her back rounded so that the gear stick would not hurt her chest too much, but he never let her do it very long; he would lift her up, and she knew then it was time to move to the back seat. Two or three times during the month of August he fucked her on the hood of the car, and she could look up at the stars. When they went back to the bar, Jean-Joseph C. left with Madeleine, and when they got back it was Xavier S. who headed out to the dirt track together with Laetitia. Everything had happened as planned. They were all in relationships with boys they had known and admired since childhood and who had watched them grow up knowing they already belonged to them, that everything was only a question of time. Now they were their women, and that was how everyone referred to them, no one used the expression "girlfriend," and rightfully so, anyway, because they had indeed become little women, in the sense of wives, at the age of sixteen or seventeen, prematurely aged, caught in the bonds of a union as rigid, starchy, and monotonous as the most predictable sort of marriage. Thus, Antonia was "Pascal B.'s woman," and this new position that totally defined her also determined the nature of her relationship with people, starting with Pascal B. himself: he treated her with an excess of devotion and respect that bordered on extreme prudishness, ruling out as a matter of principle any public displays of affection or, in private, erratic effusions of passion, to such a degree that his manner of coupling was basically just an additional sign of respect and prudishness, as if any innovation, even the tiniest, any spontaneous display of his desire was bound to be insulting and sacrilegious. Had Antonia behaved more enthusiastically as a lover, he would have found it obscene, and he went out of his way to make this inconceivable; the notion that respect and prudishness could, precisely, lead to the highest form of obscenity never even crossed his mind.

Antonia's godfather had just taken charge of several parishes, including, as he had promised himself, their village parish, and his goddaughter's love life, even if he was not aware of the carnal details, could not have distressed him more. He had nothing against Pascal B., and was sincerely saddened by his death in 1999, as by all the premature deaths of too many young people he had known and whose remains he had blessed, his wrist bending to the ever more oppressive weight of the censer—no, he had nothing against Pascal B., but he could not bear to think that Antonia's fate was already sealed, and so cheerlessly, and he felt infinitely sorry for her because he knew that the love of a man like Pascal B., a love that was sincere, clumsy, and condescending all at the same time, would invariably turn out to be toxic, and she did not know this. He wanted her to become aware of it as quickly as possible, before she had completely lost her bloom, before she had nothing left but the bitter resources of regret. He would not allow himself any moralizing remarks, he prayed for her, he prayed that God, too, would feel sorry for her and set her free, and now before her coffin, that is what he is praying for once again as he hears the melody of an unfamiliar *Kyrie eleison*. The chant begins as an almost imperceptible breath, the voices seem to be struggling against some stifling anxiety and fear in order to be heard, to break free of the earth, which they seem to do at last when after the crescendo of the first three *Kyries* the call of the *Christe eleison* fills the entire church with such perfect harmony that it breaks his heart. But with the second *Christe*, a contrapuntal voice introduces a modulation with a diminished seventh, very quietly at first, then more loudly. Marc-Aurèle has stopped weeping and is staring at the singers, aghast. The priest closes his eyes. He does not want to see his nephew's face. He should have chosen to say mass with his back to the congregation, as prescribed by the extraordinary form of the Catholic rite, to stand facing the large crucifix, and he would have simply listened to the chant, the perfect prayer, safe from the egoism so deeply rooted in the human heart that it destroys any genuine surge of feeling toward the Lord when they address him in their own words, as if speaking to a cruel, capricious despot who just might, from time to time, let himself be softened by their posturing, their servile haggling, the abject farce of their repentance, their scrupulous superstition—all of which makes them, deep down, so despicable and pitiable as they raise their fearful eyes to the heavens in hopes that God will bring the arbitrary manna of His blessings down upon them and preserve them from plagues beyond number—rivers of blood, mosquitoes and horseflies, hail, torrents of frogs and locusts, and the rain of ash that fell on the village at dawn and throughout one entire morning in September 1983.

When Antonia woke up, she saw black shapes fluttering in the sky, driven by a burning wind, falling to the ground in erratic trajectories. She went out of the house and saw that they were burned leaves, some of which had kept their shape so well that you could still see the delicate tracery of their veins before they dissolved into dust the moment you touched them. A huge fire had broken out on the rear slope of the mountain. Two villages had to be urgently evacuated. If the wind doesn't change direction, we've had it! Antonia's father said, and everyone prayed for the wind to change and send the fire toward other residences. While everyone was hoping his priesthood would guarantee him the Lord's sympathetic ear, Antonia's godfather also indulged in the same uncharitable prayer because in his distress, the fate of his other parishioners had become a matter of momentary yet complete indifference to him. The shower of ash was getting thicker, the air grew hotter and hotter, and at around noon they all gathered at the top of the village and looked at the mountain. Above them the fire-fighting planes flew back and forth, over and over, uselessly. Old women crossed themselves, weeping. Antonia had brought her camera. Can't you think of anything else at a time like this? her father asked, beside himself. I don't know why I don't go ahead and give you a good slap. She'd never seen him so angry. Not once in her entire childhood had he raised his hand against her, and it seemed unlikely he'd been waiting until she was eighteen to embark on a career as an abusive father; nevertheless, she thought it wiser to keep a safe distance. Don't worry, her godfather said. He doesn't mean what he said. Suddenly they heard a huge dull rumbling noise; the fire leapt over the crest, five hundred yards above them, and started coming down toward the village. The crackling of combustion was incredibly loud, like some apocalyptic monster roaring, a monster with a body of flame, and for the first time that morning, Antonia was afraid. She glued her eye to the viewfinder and felt better. She heard screams. In front of her, a woman turned around, mouth twisted in terror, arms raised to the sky, and set off at a run. Everyone was fleeing. Antonia pressed the shutter release a number of times. Men were weeping. She heard someone calling her name. She didn't answer and went on taking pictures. Pascal B. grabbed her by the arm. What are you doing? You have to leave! You have to leave right away! Your parents are looking for you! She tried to protest, but he dragged her by the arm, not listening, saying several times over that she was crazy, until he had brought her to her house. The able-bodied men would be staying in the village to try to save their houses with what paltry means they had. She asked to stay, too. You're going to get that slap, you know! her father screamed. Maybe even two of them! They made her get into a car with her mother and Marc-Aurèle. As they drove away from the village, she took more pictures through the open window. The village didn't burn. It remained standing, facing the sea, built right up against the blackened slope of mountain; it would take months for the brambles, maquis, and weeds to make it green again. Antonia's parents refused to look at the photographs she had taken during the fire. Pascal B. glanced at them and listlessly nodded his head in approval. Only her godfather was genuinely interested. Antonia showed him the one she thought was the best: you could see half of the screaming woman's face, her outstretched arm, her hand with its fingers spread, and behind her the wall of fire above the first houses of the village. On another one, a crouching man was weeping into his clasped hands beneath the rain of ash. Antonia's godfather borrowed the pictures and without telling her passed them on to one of his friends who worked at the local agency of their regional daily. At the end of September,

EPISTLE: FIRST LETTER OF SAINT PAUL TO THE THESSALONIANS

4

(Hanged Arabs on the Bread Market Square, Tripoli, 1911)*

M arc-Aurèle reads, his voice remarkably steady.
But I would not have you to be ignorant, brethren,
concerning them which are asleep . . .

No, we will not remain ignorant, regarding the dead. The history of photography began without movement—when the sun had to reach the end of its path across the sky above Nicéphore Niépce's estate before the strange image of walls lit from every side at once could at last be imprinted on a metal plate, along with the black outline of a fruit tree frozen in the light. Photography was bound therefore to overcome its initial timidity and evolve from the immobility of stone, dried flowers, and cannonballs to that no less perfect immobility of corpses, embalmed elders, dead children, Union soldiers on the battlefield at Gettysburg, *gardes nationaux*, and others gunned down during the Commune and laid out in rows of simple plank coffins.

By the time Gaston C. leaves Paris for Tripolitania at the end of November 1911, modern cameras have long been making it possible to freeze the motion of life. A sharp face no longer necessarily belongs to a corpse. But this simple technical progress obviously cannot undo the close ties that from the very beginning have bound photography to death.

In his luggage, Gaston C. has a Kodak film camera, lent to him by a friend. It is not due to his mediocre talent as an amateur photographer that he was chosen by *Le Matin* to cover the war Italy is waging in hopes of becoming a new colonial power. Gaston C. is a writer, and he is expected to file a detailed chronicle of the defeats of the now moribund Ottoman Empire. At the end of September, Italian troops, consisting primarily of soldiers from the South—Sardinians, Calabrians, and Sicilians— seize Tripoli. The staff expect the local population to greet them favorably or, at worst, look on the fighting with indifference. But in October, while fighting the Turks in the oasis of Sciara Sciat, the soldiers of the 11th regiment of Bersaglieri are attacked in the rear by Bedouins who chop them to pieces, as literally as possible: corpses dismembered, genitals severed, eyes gouged out. The immediate Italian reprisals are so savage that the European press, thanks to the horrified reports of a handful of correspondents at the scene, react indignantly. The Italians are confronted with an unprecedented problem: their image. Massacres and deportations have been harshly torn from the private sphere to be exposed in broad daylight. The battle of communication must be waged in the press with the help of understanding journalists invited to Tripoli. Gaston C. is one of them. He is delighted. Gaston C. adores Italy—or, to be more precise, he adores the *opéra comique* décor which, in his mind, epitomizes Italy. And he has always dreamt of the Orient—that is, in this case, a languid harem where courtesans and camels amble in the shade of huge date palms, and which, in his mind, epitomizes the Orient.

With his little Kodak in his suitcase, his heart full of joy and excitement, Gaston C. eagerly anticipates his own desires. He is not disappointed, nor could he be, for the force of his desire is such that initially he simply does not see what is there before him. The Italians are all charming, voluble, phlegmatic, and light-hearted, including the gendarmes, whom he finds irresistibly comical. The incomparable blue of the sky and sea fills him with transports of ecstasy. Every flower, every fruit, seems to have grown in the innocence of a garden of Eden; the fragrances intoxicate him, and the month of November feels like summer.

He promises his wife that one day he will share all these marvels with her.

In Messina, in Syracuse, the magic continues despite the blustery wind. On board ship, he writes proudly to his wife, he is one of the rare passengers not prevented by seasickness from frequenting the restaurant, despite the fact they serve only execrable fare washed down by even more execrable wine. A cholera epidemic prevents him from disembarking in Malta. He knows that cholera also awaits him in Tripoli, but the Italian authorities have made all the journalists bound for Libya promise not to mention it in their articles if they do not wish to be deported on the spot. Gaston C. reluctantly complies with the requirements of a censorship he considers iniquitous.

But he wants to see Africa.

His first sight is of the coast, on the morning of November 28; palm trees, mountains, desert, it is all there, and he cannot believe that this radiant sun is shining above a country at war. Together with the other accredited journalists, he is received by an extremely amiable Italian officer, who gives them an optimistic picture of the situation at the front and some fresh dates. Gaston C. walks around Tripoli, takes pictures of craftsmen, women veiled in white, stunned children playing in the dust, and for the first time he hears the muezzin calling to prayer.

He visits the Italian trenches under Turkish artillery fire. In his first article, he marvels at the sober courage of the *little soldiers*. He takes their picture, squatting in a row behind their NCO, bayonets at the ready as if they were about to charge. They do not charge, but the dark fabric of their uniforms contrasts marvelously with the white sand. The next day he goes to a zone only recently recaptured from the Turks where the corpses of twenty-four Bersaglieri from the 11th Regiment who had disappeared from Sciara Sciat have been found. They had been taken prisoner, tortured, and killed more than one month earlier. Gaston C. is deeply upset. He apologizes to the readers of *Le Matin* for having to impose the description of such horrors upon them, but they must be informed because, clearly, we must not *be ignorant concerning them which are asleep.* He describes the stitched eyelids, the severed noses. He also takes pictures that simply cannot be published, that require a certain effort of concentration to grasp what they actually represent. A soldier, the lower part of his body completely stripped, one leg bent at an impossible angle, is lying along the side of the dune. But the camera lens has erased all perspective and it is as if a mischievous demon has grabbed him by the heel and is holding him upside down, hanging in the air, like a trophy from some surreal fishing trip. A head emerges from the ground, recognizable only by its teeth. Shapeless piles lie spread across the sand, and one cannot tell fabric from parchment-like flesh, or bones from pieces of dead wood. Gaston C. goes off to breathe the desert air. He hands his camera to an officer and poses on horseback, alone against the horizon, wearing his pith helmet. He goes farther away from the Italian positions, dismounts, lies down in the sun, and gazes up at the African sky, *Oh, that sky!* he writes to his wife. When he tears himself away from his Oriental reverie, he sees the silhouettes of armed Arabs heading toward him. He leaps into the saddle and rides off at a gallop to find shelter. He tells his wife how afraid he was of being captured and how he loved that sensation of fear, his heart pounding fit to burst, the terrible, delicious dizziness of it, the joy of being alive.

He watches the airplanes take off on their way to inflict the first aerial bombardment in history upon the Turkish infantry, grenades tossed into the trenches, by hand, from the cockpit. On the way back, one of the pilots flies over the port, waves his arms, dives down toward the sea, and, grazing the waves, flies between two warships. From on deck, the sailors cheer him, shouting loudly.

On December 5, fourteen Arabs suspected of having taken part in the massacre at Sciara Sciat are led single file into Tripoli, all attached to a shared rope, their hands tied behind their backs. Gaston C. takes pictures of their arrival at the courthouse. The prisoners sit down on the tiled floor, wrapped in their long, hooded burnooses. An Italian officer reads the indictment in a language they do not understand. Above him on the wall hangs a large portrait of King Victor Emmanuel. The insurgents are all sentenced to death by hanging. On the way out of the courthouse, one of them stares at Gaston C.'s camera lens: the photographer will never forget that gaze. That night, at four o'clock in the morning, he is present at the execution on Bread Market Square, where the scaffold has been erected. His report in *Le Matin* shows irreproachable professionalism, but to his wife he writes that he did not want to try and sleep for fear of having terrifying dreams. He cannot understand the apparent indifference with which the condemned men died; nor can he understand the indifference of the crowd that gathered around the gallows where the fourteen bodies have remained hanging all day long, in the sun, amid the thick buzzing of flies, and he takes pictures of everything he cannot understand, he goes up to the hanged men, takes close-ups of their faces, he finds them *very handsome*, he is very close to them, no one comes this close. He does not look away, is not alarmed. As if under a spell, he is turned to stone. *And I still remember the face of an old man with a white beard, and the face of an adolescent.* At the end of the afternoon, he is still there when they come to take down the bodies and pile them onto a cart, he is taking pictures that resemble religious paintings, pietas, descents from the cross, and the Muslim women in their veils remind him of Mary Magdalene at the grave, he fouls up his settings, the shutter speed is too slow, despite the dazzling sun, figures are blurred, truncated, spectral, a translucent shroud floats above the ground, and on December 26, the newspaper publishes four of his photographs beneath the heading "What We Can See in Tripolitania": the fourteen Arabs in the half-dark of the war tribunal, the fourteen Arabs hanging like rosary beads from the same gallows, swaying before the eyes of a gang of impassive children, and then their bodies piled on the cart. It is impossible to know whether it was Gaston C. himself who chose the pictures and arranged them as a series, obeying not the logic of the ineluctable succession of moments in time but, rather, the logic of their simultaneity. When he looked at them, whether he was responsible or not for the particular order they were in, he must have acquired the certainty that when he was taking their picture at the military tribunal the fourteen condemned men were already dead because they already contained inside them the miserable end awaiting them at the gallows; henceforth its enormous shadow darkens their entire past life, and Gaston C. is unable to take pictures of anything other than death.

He walks around Tripoli, searches in despair for that Orient he so wanted to discover, he thinks he has caught a glimpse of it in a little shop belonging to a shoemaker, who smiles at him, he goes up to a boy sleeping by the door to the shop and stays for a moment gazing at him, smiling, too. He takes the boy's picture. He goes closer to wake him and give him a coin, gently strokes his cold shoulder. *The poor boy was dead!* he writes to his wife. *From hunger, typhus, cholera? We'll never know.* He stands motionless in the street. He doesn't understand. He is filled with rage against the Italians, who take exception to the treatment shown their own dead but allow the bodies of Arabs to rot in the street. *The thought of it still makes me weep,* he writes.

A correspondent from *Le Temps* is attacked in broad daylight by an Arab, stabbed with a knife, twice. Gaston C. reports on the event in a short article. To his wife, he describes his colleague as a braggart and a coward who deserved his misadventure. As for himself, he is sure no one will stab him because he knows how to behave around the Arabs, he does not look down on them, does not treat them harshly, he thinks these subtle things are important, and he accepts an invitation from a prominent Tripoli citizen to come around one evening, he is not afraid, or if he is afraid, he is really beginning to like it, this dizzying sensation of falling then righting oneself at the last moment; a servant is there waiting for him outside his hotel, bows to him, he follows, and once again the Orient is there before him, the moonlight above the minarets, a Moorish residence, the carpets, the priceless dishes, incense perhaps, and chests filled with gold or precious stones because Islam does not allow money to beget money, and the slaves devoted to their master, who is smoking his water pipe as he says: *Among those hanged by the Italians, there were innocent men.*

He returns to his hotel safe and sound, has no nightmares, only delightfully exotic dreams. He wakes up. He understands nothing. *How can one die in such a landscape?* he writes, again, to his wife, and he cannot come up with a coherent image of what he is experiencing, he cannot reconcile the clarity of the sky with the rotting flesh, the serenity of the desert with the slaughter, the sensual delights with the brutality, he cannot do it, he will never be able to.

In a trench a few yards away an Italian soldier receives a bullet in his chest, falters, and falls with a groan. He murmurs a few words of dialect, tries in vain to get back up, and stops struggling. His comrades begin digging his grave. *Poor Paolo!* They exchange words full of wisdom and nonchalance about the well-known brevity of human life and the virtues of resignation. Gaston C. admires their stoicism. Perhaps among these brave *little soldiers* there is one Corporal Samuele S., who, as soon as he gets back to his native region of Ogliastra, in Sardinia, will massacre the entire family, including the women and nursing children, of the man who had refused one day to give his father a glass of water. But this impassive attitude toward death of Samuele S. and his kind is not something he will ever qualify as *indifference* or *fanaticism*. Gaston C. is so far removed from everything—from the Italians, the Arabs, himself. But he has gotten closer to what he wants to show, as close as he can get, far too close, it makes him nauseous, day after day he watches as new arrivals are brought to the war tribunal, followed by yet more hangings, the same sham trial carried out with an abject good conscience beneath the portrait of the king, he takes a picture of an old man wearing a fez, and then another younger man dressed in a strange striped outfit, both of them are alive, standing between two gendarmes by the entrance to the courthouse, but Gaston C. knows very well as he presses the shutter that it isn't true, they're not alive, they're already dead, and he sees them so precisely, just as they will be two hours hence, their hands tied behind their backs, the old man still wearing his red fez, both of them hanged on the Bread Market Square, facing the indefatigable camera lens that has followed them right to the end.

Now in Paris, they wait far more eagerly for his photographs than for his articles. That is surely why he persists in inflicting upon himself the spectacle of these daily executions that are beginning to numb his heart and his soul and plunge him into a lassitude he fears he will never be able to escape. Everyone will see his photographs and, thanks to them, will know what happened here one day, the memory of those who died in Tripolitania will not disappear into the void, and no one will be able to ignore the fact that they did live. Gaston C. struggles in vain against silence and forgetting. *I do not want to seem unjust,* he writes to his wife, *either toward the Italians, or toward anyone.* But he still dreams of combat, he wants to feel the tremor of fear, not of disgust. The fighting is over. The Italians have gone to ground inside their forts after an unimpressive victory totally lacking in glory. Gaston C. asks to be sent to Benghazi, his request is turned down, he rages, he is stifling in Tripoli. On New Year's Eve, he wanders around the residence of the Italian staff members with a glass of champagne in his hand, among officers in full regalia and civilians in top hats and tails, he misses the white barracan burnooses, the fezzes, the veils. *I looked on as the Tripoli of the Barbary Coast was dying,* he writes to his wife. *A year from now all that will be left will be waiters in frock coats or funeral directors. The color of this beautiful country is vanishing.* As if to prove him right, on the morning of New Year's Day 1912, rain begins to fall on the city that is completely gray, and he feels immense nostalgia for all those things he would so have liked to know and will not know, because he arrived too late or, what is more likely, because they never existed.

He has nothing more to do in Tripolitania. He waits for the ship that will take him back to France by way of Tunis and Algiers. He takes pictures of the port. Huge wading birds on the beach. He writes to his wife that he has changed, that he feels sadder and more solid. *It is the battle of life that has given me strength, and it is I who shall give you strength.* He is proud that he did not give in altogether to the demands of Italian propaganda. *Despite their entreaties, I refused to produce the chronicles they expected of me, because I would have judged it dishonest to say what I did not think, and had I decided to say what I thought I would have had to resolve to leave this land where the slightest dissonance is christened "treason," where, whatever the cost, they want everything to be fine, even if everything is dreadful, and everything to be charming when almost everything is terrible.* He does not really care how much he has fought back, or how many compromises he has made; he does not care what his articles contain, or what figures of style or rhetorical prowess he displays. All of that has been swept away by the brutal power of the photographs.

He joins his wife in Marseille. The war is behind him. As the months go by, he recalls not the faces of the hanged men but, more and more intensely, the strange intoxication of life under fire. He has dreams where he is galloping across the desert, and the Arabs' bullets whistle past his ears like snakes he might learn to charm. He is disappointed to awake in the insipid comfort of his bedroom. The world has again become too small. He thinks about Tripoli incessantly, about Cyrenaica, which they did not let him visit. He forgets his doubts, his lassitude, his erstwhile disgust. He is seized again by the blind power of desire. He wants to set off again. The First World War will give him the opportunity. In 1915, he is appointed to the French Army's photography service on the Balkan front.

Decades later, someone will come upon Gaston C.'s photographs, all jumbled together in a cardboard box. He will see a stranger wearing a huge pith helmet, motionless on his horse in the vastness of an anonymous desert, he will see filthy children playing with pebbles in the sand, and fourteen hanged men photographed so close up that their faces can be clearly distinguished, but he will not know where, or when, or why they died.

Wherefore comfort one another with these words.

SEQUENCE: *DIES IRÆ*

5

(Members of an FLNC Commando,[2]
Ajaccio Police Station, 1984)

---

[2] National Liberation Front of Corsica (T.N.)

For the first time, in the winter of 1987, Antonia arrived at a crime scene before the police. She had been working late at the newspaper with one of her colleagues, and they'd decided to go for a drink in the old town. They had just sat down in a bar when they heard gunshots and, immediately afterward, a motorbike taking off. They ran through the deserted streets in the direction of the noise. They came upon a Jeep with broken windows. A leg was hanging out the half-open door on the driver's side. Antonia thought she could see the foot tremble slightly. The man had collapsed onto the passenger seat. The gunmen must have shot him when he was just getting into the car, or maybe he'd had time to open the door himself in one last, derisory impulse toward survival. His chest was covered in blood, and the impact from the bullets had altered his face beyond recognition. White streaks gleamed on the dark leather. Antonia took pictures of the body, the car, and the street from every angle. It was the first time she was seeing a corpse up close. She was ten years old when her grandmother died, and her parents hadn't allowed her into the room where the old lady, her face frozen for good in the doleful expression she'd worn all her life, lay on the bed where Antonia would be laid out in turn in August 2003. The policemen showed up a few minutes later and began by giving the two journalists a fierce telling-off, accusing them of having messed with the crime scene and threatening to throw them in jail to teach them not to get in other people's way. Antonia's colleague assured them they hadn't touched anything and cautiously backed away.

Aren't we going to stay for a while? Antonia asked. Don't we want to find out who it is?

I know who it is, answered her colleague, and he gave her a name she didn't recognize but that was bound to figure in the files on organized crime.

They went back to the newspaper offices. One hour later, Antonia's colleague had finished his article, but five hundred words did not add the slightest information to what was already in the headline: "Man Gunned Down in Ajaccio." As his long career in regional papers had enabled him to develop his clearly innate talent, the journalist was now cultivating the gift of empty palaver with a virtuosity that bordered on genius. He masterfully strung together commonplaces, clichés, stock phrases, and edifying opinions in such a way as to produce—without meeting any opposition and regardless of the subject—rigorously mindless texts. The article began, therefore, by pointing out that *once again, we are obliged to note that the killers' victim did not stand a chance.* The murderers' systematic lack of elegance—they obviously favored effectiveness at the expense of the most elementary rules of courtesy, and never bothered to warn their target of the imminence of his execution—was regarded each time as a regrettable lack of fair play, as if the settling of scores was supposed to be determined according to the rules of some medieval tournament among knights. The victim as usual was *known to the police for all the wrong reasons,* but they *nevertheless followed up on every lead.* The article concluded with a lyrical condemnation of violence, along with a wish for public peace to be restored in keeping with the *legitimate aspirations of our fellow citizens.*

Antonia went off to develop her photographs. At the time she took them, she had felt no particular emotion. She just knew she had to hurry before the police got there. She also had the impression her colleague was watching her, not without a certain kindness, as if in his eyes she were sitting for some strange initiatory test that he was pleased to see her passing. Only now, in the red light of the darkroom, did she see what she had shot. Looking closely at the face shattered by bullets, the gaping wound in place of a left eye, and the disgusting white streaks on the seats, she suddenly felt like throwing up. But the nausea disappeared quickly enough. She set aside those pictures they could not possibly subject readers to over breakfast and picked out one where all you could see was the Jeep, the broken glass, and the incongruous leg sticking out of the door. She had only been hired by the agency in Ajaccio a few months earlier, and she had a definite preference for covering gangland killings instead of the office parties, weddings, and official ceremonies she'd been stuck with until then. It was worth the occasional repression of a moment's nausea.

She had started work as a photographer with a little newspaper agency in 1984, when she was still "Pascal B.'s woman," which might be what convinced her employers to hire her despite her youth and total lack of experience—even if, in fact, no particular experience was required to illustrate local news items. All you had to do was stick to one basic rule, which Antonia discovered on her first day of work: the systematic use of the wide-angle lens, regardless of negative aesthetic consequences. Antonia had just come back from Nice, where she had spent an absolutely useless year at the university. There, too, everyone viewed her as the quasi-wife of a political prisoner; the milieu of Corsican students treated her with a sort of tiresome deference while keeping an eye on her slightest movements or acts, so much so that she ended up living like a solitary member of some royal family surrounded by chaperones, and she was terribly bored. She could not count on either Madeleine, who was delighted to play—to an audience of connoisseurs—the role of tearful but brave spouse, victim of the iniquity of the State, or on Laetitia, who was on the verge of publicly voicing her regret that Xavier S. had not been thrown in jail, too, for as it stood, his insignificance had deprived her of the place she felt she deserved in the whole tragedy. They've become utterly stupid, Antonia complained to her godfather, and she added that Nice was a horrible city where there were so many Corsicans that it did not even have the advantage of feeling foreign, and so, in these conditions, she added, she may as well come home rather than stay there listening to arrogant old professors give deadly dull speeches about corporate law, or the penal code, or the Constitution of the Fifth Republic. He knew he should have tried to reason with her, advise her to make an effort or at least enroll in the university in Corte that had opened two years earlier, she might switch to a course that suited her better than law, but he was incapable, the utterly disproportionate and painful compassion he felt for Antonia prevented him from seeing reason himself, and he went and sought out his journalist friend and begged him to take his goddaughter on as a photographer. He called the bar in Nice where Antonia hung out and where he could always leave a message for her if she wasn't there, but the owner of the bar put his goddaughter on the line, and when he told her the news she let out a long cry of joy. Oh, I'm so glad! And will Maman go along with it? Yes, yes, he said hastily. After hanging up, he tried to convince himself that he had not just told a shameless lie, because in his haste not for a moment had he thought of checking with his sister. Of course, it was perfectly feasible that she would congratulate him for having taken such a brilliant initiative and lend her enthusiastic approval, in which case he would be guilty only of having been one step ahead of the truth, which at worst might be considered a forgivable sin, but, as was to be expected, his sister did not approve of his idea at all and even very nearly incurred damnation for raising her hand to a man of the Church. He begged her to calm down and give Antonia a warm welcome when she came back from Nice, none of this was her fault, he alone was guilty, and he displayed all the external signs of the purest contrition. Stupid idiot! his sister said, the squirt has always had you twisted around her little finger, and you don't even realize! and he lowered his head while she shook a forefinger trembling with indignation in his face. She was about to slap him, like when they were children and he had done something wrong, and he was already about to pitifully hold out his left cheek to her after being struck on the right, when his brother-in-law came to his rescue, the voice of reason: most of the local kids who'd gone to university in recent years didn't even get any sort of degree, they just drifted from first year to first year, never set foot in class, never showed up for exams, and spent their time living it up with the money their unfortunate parents sent them; there was no reason to be sorry if Antonia could work in a field she enjoyed rather than stray like the others down the road to debauchery and perdition.

And so Antonia, armed with a professional camera and a 16-35 zoom lens, set off on her first assignment, a triples pétanque tournament in a mountain village. She had to take pictures, of course, but also record impressions of the organizers and participants, and she performed the task as seriously as if she'd been sent to cover the Yalta Conference. She immortalized a player from the victorious team in a low-angle shot just as the steel ball left his hand to make a long sparkling curve against the summer sky; she shot the awards ceremony and during the closing cocktail spoke at length with local politicians all more or less sloshed on pastis. When the head of the agency saw her work, he let out a sigh of despair. This wouldn't do at all. Antonia clearly had not understood what was expected of her, and he set about explaining it to her, calling her "sweetie" with affectionate condescension. A game of pétanque out in the country was obviously not an event likely to interest anyone apart from, notably, those who had taken part in it and who were all the more interested in it given that it was an opportunity for them to appear in the paper, and so they could cut out the article to hand the memory of that exceptional day on to posterity. Antonia's clumsiness, her wishful aesthetic self-indulgence, now deprived them of the joy they had been counting on, and you could be sure that the following day they would be calling the paper to express their disappointment, no doubt about it, and that was precisely the reason why, under these circumstances, you had to take a group photograph that included as many people as possible in the shot, starting with the mayor and the entire town council. What else was a wide angle for? Antonia, who had failed to see the rhetorical aspect of the question, began enumerating all the ways the lens could possibly and honorably be put to use, but the head of the agency didn't leave her the time to finish.

This is not a conversation, sweetie: I'm telling you how to do your work. If you want to do fancy creative stuff, do it in your time off.

With the wide angle screwed to the body, off she went to mass-produce horrible group portraits at office parties, campsite openings, beauty contests, or various commemorations, applying the director's instructions with such scrupulous zeal that she refused to change the lens when, exceptionally, she was asked to take close-ups of isolated individuals or couples. On the photographs illustrating articles entitled "They Said Yes!" or "Two 'Yesses' for One Name," the newlyweds duly deformed by the 16mm lens all seemed to have the same disproportionate nasal appendage, while their ears seemed to stretch dangerously toward the horizon, as if someone, for some obscure perverse reason, had tried to flatten their head in a vice. She shared her professional frustration with a colleague she particularly liked because unlike the other photographers at the paper he did not feel obliged to wear a sleeveless jacket adorned with an unbelievable number of useless pockets and a sand-colored scarf tied casually around the neck, which were supposed to make them look like adventurous correspondents. He had been working for the newspaper for thirty years or more and had long ago resigned himself to not expecting anything from his job. But every weekend he crisscrossed the island in search of abandoned sheepfolds, he'd photographed hundreds, granite walls, schist walls, chalk walls covered with brambles, collapsed roofs, down paths no one even remembered existed, he wanted to put a book together, he was looking for a publisher, and Antonia could not understand how anyone could subject himself to such long treks across the mountain to take pictures of abandoned piles of stones in dark desolate places, but when he showed her his work, she was struck by the aesthetic power emanating from his painstaking inventory of ruin, which spoke neither of the past nor of nature but only of humankind's ineluctable defeat. For she, too, in her free time, as the head of the agency had suggested, took her own photographs, and they painted a picture of the same defeat. She took portraits of her friends in the bar by the fireplace, where they went for drinks before dinner, their eyes fixed on the embers, or on Saturday evenings, in a stuffy deserted nightclub that smelled of stale smoke, as they leaned on the bar counter over bottles of whiskey and gin where the name of the village had been scrawled in black marker in capital letters; she captured their languor, the dreary unfolding of lives lost in the mists of an endless winter, she would wait for the moment when they went so deeply into themselves that they completely forgot her presence and that of her camera, she became invisible, and she went hunting along the village streets in search of human beings gone adrift: an old woman leaning on a walking stick next to the itinerant baker's van, two dogs by her side; a child walking along with a bag of trash in his hand, on his way to the cement container where garbage burned under a long plume of black smoke that rose in thick scrolls to the colorless sky. None of the scenes she caught on film could, strictly speaking, be said to constitute an event; the head of the agency would never agree to publish them in the paper, and yet it was these photographs, far more than the pictures of pétanque players or local administrators, that unveiled the reality of life. To Antonia this notion was very pleasing; not at all humble, she liked to picture herself as a vestal keeping the fragile flame of truth alive. But when she looked at her personal photographs, she suspected that this business about the truth was not as straightforward as it seemed. When caught by her lens, all her friends evoked characters from a tragedy, prey to unspeakable torments, which might well be the case for a young man like Simon T., but far more debatable where Laetitia O. was concerned—she had also abandoned her studies in Nice and had now given herself over to idleness—or Xavier S., whose inner life, as far as Antonia could tell, must be about as turbulent as that of an amoeba frozen in an ice floe. That was the whole problem: a total absence of tragedy, and Antonia's pictures failed to document this because they were far too heavy with a significance that was lacking all the same. Her pictures lacked innocence. It was not enough for them to capture the candid trace of the instant, and although Antonia was unable to understand why, they became part of an entire talkative and solemn network of superfluous, perhaps mendacious interpretations. At that very moment, in Turkey, there were tearful women searching for the victims of an earthquake; a car bomb was exploding in Beirut; a man was lifting a child's body toward the sky and God's undying anger; and photographers were *there*, making things *visible*, things no one wanted to see, they were not being stupidly tossed back and forth between insignificance and lies, they were useful, brave and headstrong, and Antonia, for whom Nice back then, after Ajaccio, represented the northernmost limits of the known world, dreamt of being with them and struggling with them against the comfort of ignorance. From time to time, a night of bombings or mob violence gave her the opportunity to produce some authentic journalism, but such events were few and far between, and all she brought back were shots of no particular interest—ruined holiday homes, or gendarmes leaning over a body she could not get closer to.

Her new profession, however unsatisfactory, did allow her at least to gain her independence much sooner than she would have imagined. She left the village and her childhood bedroom for an apartment in town, and she bought a secondhand car which she claimed to have obtained on credit when in fact it was her godfather who had secretly bought it for her. She meticulously decorated her bedroom, where she burned incense, and she pictured herself lying in cool, clean sheets next to Pascal B. on the day he'd get out of prison. When in May 1985 Antonia heard he was about to be released, together with Jean-Joseph C., she burst into tears right there in the agency. The boss and all his colleagues came to hug her, and her tears flowed even faster. She had been waiting for Pascal for nearly two years, and now that he was due to land in Ajaccio the following day at the latest, it seemed to her she could not wait another minute. But the longest hours do eventually go by, and together with Simon, Madeleine, who had rushed back from Nice, Laetitia, and Xavier, she was soon driving to Campo dell'Oro to the arrivals hall, where over-excited militants were singing and waving Moor's head flags, and they all cheered in unison when the airplane doors opened, Antonia could just make out the passengers crossing the tarmac, she tried to spot Pascal, but she couldn't see a thing, the crowd was shoving her this way and that, and suddenly there he was, a few yards away, held by unknown arms, and he waved to her and winked at her, and she stood petrified in the tumult of her racing heart until at last he came over to her, stroked her cheek, and placed a kiss on her eyelids.

That evening they all met up at a restaurant on the mountain where, to celebrate Pascal B.'s return in a dignified manner, they would serve him all the specialties he'd been deprived of for so long. He was euphoric. He drank a lot. Before the end of the apéritif, he leaned over to whisper to Antonia. Come with me. I can't wait anymore. They left the dining room, and a few knowing gazes watched them, which made Antonia feel uncomfortable. They drove through a pine forest carpeted with tall ferns undulating in the spring breeze, the moon was full, Antonia thought about her apartment, impeccably tidy and fragrant, the white sheets on her bridal bed, but she said nothing, she didn't want to spoil Pascal's first day of freedom on the pretext that it was not going exactly how she would have liked. Come. He pulled her onto the back seat and kissed her with a rough, coarse passion, and, not leaving her the time to respond to his embrace or return his caresses, he slipped a feverish hand under her dress and brutally rammed his finger into her vagina. At first Antonia tried to calm him down, release him from his clumsiness, she did not tell him he was hurting her, she murmured as quietly as she could, wait, please, wait a minute, but he was shaking his head convulsively, he was licking her ear, smearing her with saliva, I can't take it anymore, you have no idea, I really can't take it anymore. His voice was trembling, and Antonia could not tell which was more vulgar, that trembling voice or the words it was saying, she tried to push him off, never abandoning her gentle approach, saying again, wait, kiss me, but he didn't even hear her anymore, and he penetrated her, yanking aside the elastic on her panties. Antonia stopped struggling. She felt betrayed by the docility of her body, which offered itself limply, she heard herself moaning while the remarkable vulgarity of this man's voice, full of a desire that showed no concern for her, blew to smithereens all her dreams of incense, tenderness, and white sheets, and a few seconds later Pascal B. climaxed, letting out a cry she would rather not have heard, and she closed her eyes for no reason while he slumped heavily on top of her. She got out of the car. He lay there for a moment longer, then came to join her. He hunted for his cigarettes. He was smiling. She burst into tears before she had even become aware of her sadness. He seemed stunned. He asked what was wrong and tried to take her in his arms, but she pulled away, making no further attempts to be gentle, she buried her face in her hands, tears running through her fingers, she sobbed, and the silent forest, the moonlight reflected by the ferns, the jagged outline of the Aiguilles de Bavella on the horizon, all seemed sad to her and frozen in the eternal, disdainful indifference of time, she wanted to keep her eyes closed, to forget the moment, to forget this man she did not know and who had at last understood that something was wrong and had now come to her saying he was sorry and this time she did not have the strength to push him away. He had thought about her for too long, too sorrowfully, he'd wanted her so much, I want you so bad, he said with conviction, and this cliché from a lover's vocabulary disgusted her, he was incapable of finding words for her, which in the end was better, because she knew that if he had tried to make the slightest effort to be inventive, it would have been even worse, so much so that she'd rather he said absolutely nothing and let her cry, but he would not let her, he was right there next to her, he was telling her he loved her, as if this were the right moment to make this confession she had waited such a long time for, and when she looked at him, he was so clearly confused and defenseless that he looked like a little boy and she took him in her arms and told him she loved him, too, that she had always loved him. I don't want us to do it in the car. Ever again. All right, he replied. They went back to the restaurant, and at the end of the evening he embraced his parents and went to sleep at Antonia's place.

Now he spent the night there several times a week, and this was what it meant to be an adult, not having an apartment or a salary, but simply sleeping with Pascal B. in a bed rather than on the back seat of a car, which proved not only to be more comfortable but above all more gratifying because he always called to ask if he could come, and even if she invariably said yes because she never stopped waiting for him, she appreciated the fact he showed her consideration in this way by treating her at last—although nothing obliged him to—like an individual with her own free will. For Antonia, this source of satisfaction was anything but trifling, particularly as her life hardly offered her anything better. She still went to the nightclub of her teenage years every weekend, which suddenly, at the beginning of the summer of 1985, began playing shockingly horrible music; she sat in the same old booth with Laetitia and Madeleine, who by now had also given up on her studies and confessed to Antonia, screaming in her ear to make herself heard while glancing worriedly over at the bar where Jean-Joseph C. was drinking, that in Nice she'd had an affair with a grad student. The guy wasn't from Corsica, fortunately, they had no friends in common, she had met him at the library, one of the rare times, perhaps the only time, she'd set foot in the place, and she slept with him one hour after their initial encounter, while Jean-Joseph was still in prison, she had wept all day long the following day, she felt horribly guilty, and yet she saw the guy again several times, she didn't get it, why, as time went by, did the guilt become easier to bear, then almost imperceptible, until all that remained was the desire to see him again and to sleep with him again, a terrible desire that was all the more imperious in that it was absolutely devoid of any sentimental dross, and she would go and knock on the door at his studio, not giving him the time to say a word, and when she awoke in the morning she was horrified by the intensity of her transports of lust and by the untapped resources of her depraved imagination, she was crushed by guilt, it was unbearable, she would run away, and this had gone on for months, until last week, because when she went to get her things at the university dorm, she couldn't help but go and see him, swearing of course that it would be the last time but not believing a word of it, so that in the end the only way for her to get out of it and make sure that this time really was the last was to never go to Nice again. I behaved like a slut, concluded Madeleine, screaming to make herself heard as best she could. What? shouted Antonia. I'm a slut, Madeleine said again. Antonia assured her that she was not a slut, she didn't judge her, but she had nothing else to offer besides the abstract smile of her compassion because she couldn't understand that one's own body could be the locus of such torment, and she couldn't get herself interested in it. All that mattered to her was her professional future. She shivered at the thought that twenty or thirty years down the road she might still be working for the same agency and have become so used to taking mediocre photographs that she would not even notice it anymore and might actually be ridiculously proud of her work. In July, the FLNC decided to hold a press conference in the region, thus giving Antonia an unprecedented opportunity to do some reporting worthy of the name. One evening she was on a back road together with a colleague from the paper and a team from the regional television channel. A van pulled up next to them. The door opened, and a man in military fatigues and a balaclava motioned to them to get in. Antonia sat with her colleagues. She put on a blasé expression to hide the fact she was actually excited to be having this great adventure, but then she dropped her tripod on the ground. The militant picked it up and handed it back to her. He stared at her, and she got the impression that beneath his balaclava he was smiling at her. She murmured her thanks, timidly. Don't mention it, he replied politely. She instantly recognized Simon T.'s voice and suspected that he had only spoken so that she would know it was him. The van came to a halt. Simon T. motioned to the journalists to follow him, and they headed down a path into a clearing. Beneath a Corsican flag hanging from a tree branch, a militant was sitting at a table with a paper in his hand, surrounded by a dozen or so armed men. He began reading the text of the press release, and this time Antonia recognized Pascal B.'s voice, in spite of the ludicrous effort he was making to disguise it. As she took her pictures, she realized she was bound to know every one of those faces hiding behind a balaclava, and what ought to have seemed to her like the privilege of being initiated to the Mysteries was now deeply depressing. All the joy she should have felt at accomplishing a worthwhile task had vanished. It was not the thrilling history of an island in the Mediterranean she was a part of, this was just some puerile game where old childhood friends dressed up as fighters and journalists without even managing to take their respective roles seriously. She was taking pictures of bad actors reciting the incredibly pompous text of a failed play that neither violence nor years in prison could render more authentic, and Antonia was just playing a part, like the others, her acting perhaps even crappier than theirs. Every time she pressed the shutter release, she was validating this production that had nothing to do with reality but existed merely in the expectation of being transformed into images. None of it seemed the least bit honorable. Moreover, if you really thought about it, the overwhelming majority of photographers did not practice an honorable profession, they gave importance to futile subjects or, worse yet, they manufactured futility, and if on top of it they had any artistic pretensions, that made it even worse—the meanest family portrait, no matter how blurry or poorly centered, was worth infinitely more than most press photographs—never mind advertising or fashion, where all the limits of ignominy had been shamelessly exceeded, so that in the end the most prestigious magazines were nothing more than despicable rags, even more revolting than the local daily Antonia was probably doomed to work for her whole life long. In Lyon, a trial was about to be held of the FLNC commando that in June 1984 had burst into the prison in Ajaccio to execute Jean-Marc L. and Salvatore C., who had been responsible for the kidnapping and assassination of Guy O., who was himself a militant and the treasurer of the organization Antonia found increasingly difficult to qualify as clandestine. Terrifying rumors circulated about Salvatore C., a torturer and killer who, so people said, was in the habit of feeding the mangled bodies of his victims to the pigs. Antonia had a look at the investigation file Pascal B. had managed to obtain, in all probability through a lawyer. There were photographs of corpses on the beds in their cells. Jean-Marc L. was wearing striped pajamas. His hands and feet were curved back like claws. The autopsies were also painstakingly documented. Skulls had been sawn through, ribcages opened, their viscera laid out in broad daylight, long rods penetrated the bullet wounds, surgical steel gleamed, and the forensic pathologist solemnly held out to the camera lens the pale mass of a brain as if he were showing the world the pitiful material nature of life. Antonia looked closely at the photographs, feeling no particular disgust, because it was almost impossible to imagine these slabs of meat had once been put together to make up a human body. The photographs that fascinated her showed living people, commando members immediately after their arrest standing in a row in front of a white wall: Pierre A., Pantaléon A., and Bernard P. had broken into the jail disguised as gendarmes; Jean-Dominique V. and Georges M. had been arrested outside. At that very moment they were probably expecting to spend the rest of their lives in prison, or if not their entire lives, anything that remained of their youth. They were staring straight at the camera, their gazes full of haughtiness and resignation with, perhaps, a touch of pride or defiance, a gaze so intense and poignant that Antonia could not look for long without tears welling in her eyes. The gaze of the defeated looking at their enemy. They had no hopes, no regrets, they were admirable in their failure, far more so than they would have been had the operation been a success and no one had ever seen their faces. There was no trickery, no staging of the scene, just the power of truth. A policeman who knew nothing about photography had taken this unforgettable photograph simply because he happened to be there at the right time. Antonia asked to be sent to Lyon to cover the trial. She was told that it was impossible for two reasons, both of them prohibitive: no photography was allowed during hearings at the criminal court, something Antonia hadn't known, and even had that not been the case, they would not have picked her to cover such an important event. She took some vacation time and left for Lyon with Pascal B., Simon T., and other militants from the region. During the trip, she thought bitterly that no one would have thought of sending Pascal B. to the prison in Ajaccio; like her, they only entrusted him with trifling assignments: it meant they were particularly well matched as a couple. When he sat down next to her in the courthouse in Lyon, he put his hand on her shoulder, staring at the dock where the accused would be sitting. She could sense his fervor, the utter sincerity of his faith, and she reproached herself for acting so unkindly toward him. The defendants entered the room. Throughout the entire trial Antonia imagined the pictures she would have taken if some stupid rule had not forbidden her—Pierre A. reading the text of a joint declaration, the prosecutor asking for life, the ermine, the scarlet gowns, the black gowns, the prosecutor Antoine S. reciting to the jury the lines of some ancient call for vengeance, vibrant with inexpiable hatred, it was not enough for the murderers to be killed, clouds of ravens must also devour their flesh and leave them unburied amid the iniquity of their bare bones so that on Judgment Day they would not be able to take part in the resurrection, the tears of the lawyer Marie-José B. when the judge handed down sentences ranging from three to eight years of prison, the incredulous defendants in the dock trying to contain their joy, and Antonia wondered which of these faces had been the last one Jean-Marc L. and Salvatore C. had seen when they were dragged from their sleep that day, that day of anger, the face of the man who was about to become a murderer like them, and whose voice said, "Guy O. sent us," leaving them just time enough to realize they would not be forgiven because God's mercy cannot tarnish His justice and those who are cursed are doomed to the bitter flames of hell, and perhaps on that morning in June 1984 it wasn't the face of a man they had seen, but that of the king of terrible majesty bringing his punishment down upon them and reserving redemption and grace for others, while in his hand he held the severed head with its hair of snakes whose gaze met their blind eyes and whose terror crushed their hearts of ash just before the shots rang out in the prison corridors, the way they had rung out in Antonia's ears in the little streets of Ajaccio's old town in the winter of 1987, and would ring out more and more often in the years to come. The prisoners were led away. Antonia and her friends went for a drink in a bar near the courthouse. Pascal B. was euphoric. He never thought the sentences could be so light. The FLNC had drawn up plans to organize the commando's escape, on the assumption that the sentence was bound to be longer than ten years. Now such a plan was no longer necessary. Antonia still thought with regret of all the pictures she could have taken. She sat there in silence, then suddenly leaned over to Simon T., next to her in the booth.

Honestly, was it really asking too much for you to keep your mouth shut?

What? he said, not understanding.

On the day of the press conference, Antonia said, couldn't you have kept your mouth shut? Didn't it occur to you that there are things that don't interest me at all and that I don't want to know?

She was deliberately being mean. She spoke quietly so the others would not hear, but that day the voice that Simon T. will never hear again was trembling with anger and indignation.

Simon is sitting just below Our Lady of the Rosary. He is holding himself stiffly on his chair in the sweltering church. Sweat is pouring down his face, burning his eyes, soaking his clothes. Sometimes a faint puff of air makes him shiver. He has listened to seventeen tercets of the endless *Dies iræ*, the repeated alternation of two melodic lines. The chant ends with three distichs that come to break the monotony of the ensemble. One voice continues alone, on a very high note, *Lacrimosa dies illa—Tearful will be that day, on which from the glowing embers will arise the guilty man who is to be judged.* Simon doesn't believe Antonia is guilty of anything, nor that she will rise again from the ashes. She'd been right to be angry with him. What he'd done had been ridiculously childish. In the van, he was proud of his balaclava, proud of the gun he was carrying in his belt, proud like an idiot. He'd been unable to resist the temptation of showing off to her, to make her see, against all expectations, that he did look a little like Pascal B., the man he admired so much and who had everything that he, Simon, could never have—universal respect, the glory of prison, and Antonia's love. He'd just wanted to say to her, you see, I'm here, too, because it was the only thing he had the right to say to her. But he'd made her angry, honestly, was it asking too much for you to keep your mouth shut? and her anger left him feeling helpless and hurt, he felt trapped, there in the booth in that bar in Lyon, he couldn't run away, he was afraid Antonia would realize how much it hurt and realize that it wasn't because of some simple wounded pride, and he looked down and murmured something in apology, words he now repeats as he looks at her coffin, I'm sorry, Antonia, I am truly sorry.

GOSPEL: JOHN 11: 21–27

6
(Ball on Saint Roch's Day, Alta Rocca, 1973)

whom, like Lazarus, resurrection has been promised. Antonia's godfather recalls that when he was a child, these stories about resurrection left the old people feeling skeptical. His grandmother, who nevertheless made sure he said his daily prayers and spent his time between church and cemetery, did not believe in it. It was not that she suspected the priest of lying, but rather of allowing himself to be carried away by an excess of enthusiasm, if he imagined that the privilege of eternal life, no doubt reserved for men of God, would also be granted to common mortals. He'll resuscitate, she said, but we won't. If the dead survived, it was in the form of frightening, jealous, amnesiac ghosts, who haunted the riverbanks at nightfall and required payment for their favors. All those sanctimonious old women, deep down, had never turned their back on paganism, they believed that God and supernatural forces had to be treated with care to fend off the misfortunes of life on earth and, of all those misfortunes, death was precisely the one that offered neither consolation nor the possibility of rescue: that was why they wished it upon their enemies. From the time he had spent with them, Antonia's godfather had come away with a certain wariness where words of consolation were concerned. In the course of his years in the priesthood, he had seen the mass transformed inexorably into a psychological support cell, and he had heard priests outdo each other with sickly sweet homilies—transforming misfortune into happiness by means of shameful conjuring tricks, as if death could be treated lightly, if not purely and simply denied, as if it were cause for rejoicing. He does not want to deny death. He does not want to speak words of consolation: their obscenity disgusts him. Whenever he has had to prepare his homily for the service for the dead, he has been careful not to tone down the ambiguity of the biblical text, for neither the Scriptures nor even the liturgy present death as some amiable pleasantry, even if efforts had been made to remove all the texts describing dread and

trembling—the *Dies iræ,* the *Libera me*, which he insists on
having sung or recited because he refuses to allow people to be
treated like children. During the 1990s, he buried three young
men, murdered all three, Pascal B. among them, and when he
had first taken up his parish on the mainland three years earlier, he'd had to celebrate the funeral mass of a little five-year-
old girl who'd been hit by a car, and he'd spent all the previ-
ous night praying, he would have liked to leave out his homily,
not to have to say a single word of his own, open his mouth
only to say what was prescribed, because who wants to be con-
soled when the Lord Himself is in tears? But then the dreadful
moment arrives when it is no longer possible to hide from the
rite, there before the congregation, there before the departed,
one must say out loud the awkward words one chose in solitude, never knowing whether they will sound too melodra-
matic or, on the contrary, too offhand, when it would be infinitely easier to go on reading the Gospel, for its text does not
stop, obviously, with the proclamation of eternal life. After
Martha, Jesus comes upon Mary. She throws herself at his feet,
she weeps, he is troubled and trembles and begins to weep as
well, as if he has forgotten that Lazarus will soon rise from the
grave and therefore there is no reason to be mournful. As a
boy, at catechism, Antonia's godfather was offended by what
he considered then to be a blatant error of elementary logic.
Since he's going to raise him from the dead, why is he crying?
he asked. His priest at the time seemed embarrassed. He ven-
tured confused replies, none of which were satisfactory
because he was not a great theologian, and since his pupil kept
asking, he ended up imposing silence upon him, denouncing
the boy's harmful skeptical tendencies which would surely
cause his ruin. After his first communion, Antonia's godfather
declared he did not want to go to catechism anymore, and
despite his mother's threats he initially refused to go back on his
decision until they told him that if he continued in his stubborn

ways he would also have to give up serving mass. He could not bring himself to stop being a choirboy, he liked his white alb, the meticulous repetition of the same gestures, the heavy scent of incense. So he yielded to their pious blackmail and continued his Christian education, asking no more questions, although he still felt cheated. Nowadays he believes that, during the night of terrible solitude in the garden of Gethsemane, neither Christ's tears nor his desperate plea to have the cup pass away from him are hiding any errors of logic or contradiction that ought to be reduced or skipped over, because the God become man is now torn and suffering, and what would have been human about him if he had spared himself the experience of fear and despair? The priest stands to give the homily. The speech he has prepared unravels, he can't remember what he wanted to say, he just thinks, we, too, we know that she is close to the Lord, and we weep for her all the same, but he does not say it. He looks at his sister, his brothers, his brother-in-law, his nephew, and the coffin, he is not ashamed of his inner trembling, and he says, Jesus will raise Lazarus from the dead, but, just before the miracle, he weeps, and this may surprise us because, after all, he who is the resurrection and the life, why is he weeping? He tries to explain, he says that these tears emerge from the very heart of Christianity, and he thinks that his position is impossible, one never knows how to behave with the dead, nor how much distance one should take from them, there is probably no appropriate distance, when we do not know them, we must avoid sticking to the banal utterances that are always inspired by laborious compassion and try, rather, to capture the dead in their imperfect singularity, and when we know them, we must not surrender to the lyricism of our sorrow, must not let the uncle and godfather speak in lieu of the priest, deep down we always usurp something, the grief of the families, the priestly robes, there's no way out, the best would probably be not to wonder, to always repeat the same thing just changing the name, Your servant, who lived in the hope of Your light, from the baptismal waters to their death, You were there with them all their life, they listened to Your word, followed Your commandments, they loved You and had faith in You, as if only saints were ever laid to rest, when that is not true, the dead are not saints, he thinks, any more than the living are, and Antonia did not live in the hope of Your light because she did not love You, to be honest, she hated You and only conceded You might exist in order to ask you to make sense of the world and shower You with criticism, except, he thinks, it was not You she was showering with criticism but me, and no matter how often I told her it was not my job to explain suffering but simply to try to relieve it, she was angry with me because not only was I not explaining anything but also, on top of it, I was not relieving anything either, she said it spitefully, to hurt me because she was angry, but she was right, in a way, I really was incapable of relieving suffering, at least her suffering, and when she got back from Yugoslavia she eventually couldn't stand me anymore at all, faith for her was no longer an error or a naïve trait you might, at a push, make fun of, it was a moral failing, a disgrace, the symptom of culpable, monstrous blindness, but there's no sin in that, the weakness of a heart filled with love is not a sin in Your eyes, and that is why I know she is near You, even if I'm weeping for her all the same, he thinks as he makes his way as best he can through his homily, getting muddled in subtle exegeses that no one understands, his sister's black gaze trained on him as if he were the most incompetent of all the Flemish Franciscans, he ought to put an end to this disaster, at least make an effort to say Antonia's name, but he doesn't know how to conclude, no one is placing the burning coal of deliverance and purity upon his lips, and now he's forcing the congregation to cross with him to the other side of the brook Cedron, in the Gardens of Gethsemane. He again regrets he yielded so foolishly to his sister's insistent request, he is even almost sorry he ever responded to the call of the priesthood, which should not have been addressed to him. What had he accomplished other than to mortally wound all those who once loved him, starting with Antonia? She had been such a loving child, he recalls, and briefly interrupts his speech to hold back his tears but does not say her name, and she is running toward him, look at me, look at me dancing! She is eight years old, it's the village feast, on St. Roch's Day, the schoolyard is surrounded by a wattle fence, the band, more or less off-key, is playing a passionate tango in the heat of the August night, *Let me pick your lips like a flower,* Antonia's godfather is leaning against the wooden counter, and behind it bottles of champagne are floating amidst blocks of ice in huge green garbage cans, couples are dancing, deadly serious and dressed to the nines in cashmere shirts, dresses, high heels clicking on the cement, *Come and dance, life's too bitter, other arms will make you forget me,* Pascal B. and his friends are between twelve and fifteen years old, they are drinking that awful Get 27 with manly stoicism, Xavier S. goes to one side to throw up as discreetly as possible, a thick green liquid stinking of mint, but the younger children, in pairs, are also dancing the tango, imitating the adults, stifling their laughter, shoving everyone, and sometimes, with a certain ease, they frantically accelerate their pace in order to dodge the indignant, slower dancers who attempt to kick them in the behind, Look at me dancing! Antonia's left hand squeezing Simon T.'s right hand, he's eight years old, too, their free arms looped around each other's waists, and they're crisscrossing the dance floor every which way to the rhythm of the music, cheek to cheek, chins thrust forward, *Tomorrow, my darling, we won't be dancing together.* Out of the corner of her eye she makes sure she has all her godfather's attention while he watches her, half-drunk, with a smile. On the opposite side of the dance floor, sitting alone at a table, is Damienne T., Simon's

mother, also watching the children. Antonia's godfather heads
over to her. He pauses to toss some wrinkled banknotes on the
counter. He brings over a bottle of champagne in a bucket. He
chats with her for a moment and invites her to dance. She hes-
itates for a second. Since her husband died on a high-voltage
line three years earlier, she hasn't danced with anyone at the
village feast. She's thirty-five years old. On her pale face, her
lips are barely colored. She is neither beautiful nor particularly
ugly, simply dull, faded. Antonia's godfather suddenly gets the
impression that right at the very heart of that dullness, beneath
her diaphanous skin, he can see something gleaming, something infinitely poignant, a fragile flame. She gets up, and he
follows her onto the dance floor. They take a few steps, and
Antonia and Simon come over to them and cling to them with
all their weight, and all four of them dance together, staggering. *Don't go away, let me still believe, it was all a dream, and
you're still mine.* They are briefly dazzled by the glare of a flash
bulb. The tango comes to a halt. The band launches into a
series of rock numbers, then slower dances, then in keeping
with an unchanging cycle, a new series of tangos and paso
dobles. It is five o'clock in the morning. Xavier S.'s father has
just found his son sprawled in a bush. He slaps him, shouts at
him to wake him up. Simon has fallen asleep beside his mother
while Antonia is trying to keep her eyes open. But she doesn't
object when her parents tell her it's time to go home. For a long
moment she curls her arms around her godfather's neck and
lays her head on his shoulder to wish him good night. I'm
going home, too, Simon's mother says. I'll see you back,
Antonia's godfather suggests. I'll carry the boy, no point waking him up. They walk through the village streets. In the east
the stars are no longer visible. When they come to her house,
she does not invite him in but goes ahead herself and leaves the
door open behind her. He follows her to Simon's bedroom and
lays the little boy down on his bed. He leaves her to tuck him

in. He could say good night and go home but he waits in the living room. A cat rubs against his legs, purring. On the wall there are the usual portraits of old people and soldiers. Damienne's wedding photo stands on the buffet next to another one, probably taken at the maternity hospital where, all pale, she is holding her baby in her arms. She comes back into the room, walks toward him. She looks at him attentively, and now he thinks she is beautiful. Shyly, she moves closer. She puts her arms around his neck and, like Antonia, places her head on his shoulder. She raises her head and tries to kiss him, but he evades her kiss, holding her closely. He's afraid of the photographs looking at them. She leads him into the bedroom. He looks around anxiously for the eyes of the dead husband but sees only the peeling wallpaper and some dust on the night table. She takes off her dress. Her skin is not like that of the handful of girls he's known from cabarets or nightclubs, or after poker games, it is looser, rougher, completely white, with imperceptible marbling at the edge of her breasts, in the fold of her groin, like a rough draft of the decline to come, and he is moved by it. The daylight has lit up a corner of the room. He lies on top of her, he sees her black eyes shining, she bites his shoulder, soundlessly, and, again, as he moves backward, she puts her arms around his neck. As long as he stays with her, she will repeat this gesture, and he will end up believing that sexuality is nothing more than a strange pathway leading to this instant of perfect chastity. She doesn't let him fall asleep. I don't want you to leave, but you have to, she murmurs. Because of Simon. He gets up and gets dressed, and when he goes out, he is dazzled by the sun. He walks for a moment through the village streets, there is still the enchantment of first mornings, and the months go by and he no longer has to leave before Simon wakes up, there are no more secrets to share, the photographs withdraw into their inertia, are no longer threatening, but when he looks at Damienne's face, a fragment of beauty he alone can see still flickers beneath her pallor like the flame of the candle, even though two years have gone by, he wakes up, Damienne's arms around his neck, and he feels a pang of anguish, he doesn't know what to do with his useless emotion, he is distant, silent, unhappy with himself, he wishes she would find fault with him for his silence, his indifference, because if she did, he could tell her he does care about her and he cannot understand why the love he feels for her is so clearly sterile, but he says nothing, he goes out a lot, plays cards, comes back late without warning, and she never finds fault with him for anything. One winter night, the poker game ends at two o'clock in the morning. He puts the money he has won in his pocket and offers everyone a round. He looks for the friend who was supposed to drive him back up to the village. They tell him he left an hour ago. He's sorry to hear that. He supposes he ought to take a hotel room in town, but he's not tired, and besides, in this season and at this time of night he won't find a room, so he says good night to everyone and begins the long six-mile walk back up to the village. He walks through the darkness, his hands in his pockets. He's tired. He has a feeling someone is following him. He turns around from time to time to peer into the night. His heart is racing. Leaving on foot was a crazy idea. Eventually he walks past the gate to the cemetery. There is a light on in the window in the house of the old priest who didn't like questions. There are plenty of possible reasons why an old man would have the light on in the middle of the night—insomnia, senility, his prostate—but Antonia's uncle immediately thinks, with the indisputable authority of certainty, he's dead, and he becomes fixed on this idea for all that it is fragmentary, incomplete, demanding a conclusion that does not come, he struggles against the obvious, says again, he's dead, the priest is dead, and he wonders what comes next, he's dead and now what? He says it out loud, and now what? The answer is almost there but keeps slipping away until suddenly the sentence is complete: the priest is dead, and you are going to take his place. He is dumbfounded, honestly, tonight he's having nothing but insane thoughts and this one is particularly insane, but he can't shake it off. He goes on home, not making a sound. He lies down next to Damienne and falls asleep almost immediately. It's mid-morning when she wakes him up. She hands him the coffee she's made him. Do you know what happened last night? He answers, yes, I know. The priest died. She looks at him. Who told you that? He doesn't answer. He says, the priest died, and I'm going to take his place. She laughs. He would like to laugh along with her, he cannot, this absurd foreign notion has taken root and is spreading through him like a tumor, and the more he struggles against it, the weaker he feels, he yields to it, again he protests, I don't even believe in God, but he doesn't know anything anymore, do I believe in God, in the end? he asks, when that question already has no meaning anymore because what is happening to him has nothing to do with what he believes or doesn't believe, it isn't some intellectual conversion but a brutal abduction, with no going back, the brand of the burning coal on his lips, his bones broken, the suffering, his eyes blind on the road to Damascus. One spring morning, still in bed, he hears Damienne and Simon having breakfast in the kitchen. The cat jumps on the bed. He strokes it. A warm light is seeping into the room through the blinds. He looks at the cat purring beside him, its eyes half closed, and he begins to weep because everything is finished and never again will he experience the domestic sweetness of a morning like this. There are no more questions, no more doubts. He goes into the kitchen. I'll be going away, he says, and Damienne knows exactly what he means. She nods her head, looks exhausted. He goes over to Simon, squats down. We'll see each other again soon, you know, I'm not abandoning you. He cannot decipher the little boy's serious gaze. When he has closed the door behind him, he weeps again, weeps for the life that, for all that, he no longer wants and that will never return, weeps for the cowardice of his final lie, I'm not abandoning you, of course he is, of course he's abandoning him, he's abandoning both of them to answer the call of a voice that resounded in the night and that he initially thought was his, and he is guilty, even if he had no other choice than to answer that call, he is guilty, and nothing can make up for that. He runs to the deserted church. He falls to his knees in the central aisle, opposite the cross. Our Lady of the Rosary is holding her beads out to him. Tears are the only prayer he can say. Once he has dried them, he goes to his sister's place. He calls the bishopric. I would like to be received by His Grace. He does not even know the bishop's name. Throughout the joy of his years at the seminary, he carries the burden of his sin, he is still carrying it today in the church when he catches a glimpse of Damienne, an old woman, so old now, seated near the central aisle, listening to his pitiful homily. Perhaps she is thinking: was it all worth it, just to become such a bad priest? Is he such a bad priest? In any case that is what they must be thinking, the faithful gathered there on whom he is inflicting an interminable homily after first putting them through the entire *Dies iræ*, in this heat wave that has transformed the church into a furnace, perhaps some of them will feel unwell, others might eventually leave, unable to stand another minute, but let them leave, he thinks, let them all leave, let them leave me alone with Antonia, he thinks, still talking, *My soul is exceeding sorrowful*, no one is listening to him, he sees them wavering in the heat and slumping in the pews, *What, could ye not watch with me one hour*, let them leave then, they only came in order to be seen, so they would register who was there and who was missing, they're fulfilling their social obligation, with no great enthusiasm, and now they're trapped, their compassion cannot withstand one hour of discomfort, it's too much to ask, they're sinking into the incurable mediocrity of their selfishness, and if they try to escape, their sin plunges them into it again, he thinks, oh, I know you, I know all of you, because I'm like you, I know it very well and of course I would not judge you so harshly if the poor body that has to endure the insult of your weariness today were not that of my sweet little niece. He knows them all, it's true, he's lived with them, baptized the youngest among them, he married Laetitia O. to that dark idiot Xavier S. who is conspicuously wiping his brow and snorting like a beast at the trough, he has even heard confession from some of them, and they were careful not to confess their true sins precisely because they, too, knew him only too well and felt ashamed in his presence, so much so that they accused themselves profusely of specific yet minor, abstract sins, not only abstract but also completely imaginary, the way he himself used to do before his first communion when he had to make confession to the old priest who'd watched him grow up, and to whom, before even receiving the host, he would hypocritically recite, his tone falsely contrite, a list of sins straight out of a preparatory manual for children, I did not say my evening prayer on purpose, I fought with my brothers, I had bad thoughts about my parents, careful never to evoke the unbearable concupiscence that twisted his guts and plunged him into compulsive throes of masturbation, or the heady delight of swearing every chance he got and beating his classmates black and blue. All those years spent among people who had been so close to him for so long had almost managed to convince him that the sacrament of confession must inevitably be tainted by falsehood, until he moved to the mainland where he was among parishioners who did not know him and who made confession to him with an openness he sometimes found excessive and that troubled him so greatly that he sometimes dreamt of the charms of a monastic life. He knows very well that if the love of one's neighbor were that easy, Christ would certainly not have bothered to make it one's primary obligation. Antonia's godfather constantly struggled to tame his will through prayer, in order to practice as best he could the love of these neighbors whose whispering voices in the shadows painted a revolting picture of human baseness, ambition, mediocre jealousy, pettiness, greed, selfish pleasure and sordid desire, the sweatiness of daily petty crimes, sin without brilliance like the dead eye of a snake. Seated in the confessional, he felt as if he were floundering in a cesspool. Every month, the same old man would confess to him how he had a great-niece who regularly spent the weekend at his place so he would not be all alone, and how he would spy on her as she stepped out of her shower. How his cataract-clouded eye followed the droplets trickling down the young woman's body as she wrapped herself in a towel, how he waited for the moment when the falling towel might reveal the damp nudity he had caressed a hundred times over in the perverse intimacy of his dreams, forgive me, Father, if you only knew how sorry I am, every month this old man, in addition to absolution, received the vigorous exhortation to mend his ways, but the following month he was back again, enriching his story with some new, even viler detail—collecting pubic hair from the shower stall, a hole pierced in the door with a hand drill, until Antonia's godfather began to think that none of it was true and that this man took as great a pleasure in telling the imagined tale of the sin he dared not commit as in accusing himself of it, until the priest began to wonder if by listening so carefully he had not become an unwitting accomplice in a double blasphemy and was not, moreover, encouraging its recurrence. He did not accuse his parishioner of lying but eventually refused to give him absolution. It doesn't work like that, he said harshly, your soul is not some dish towel you can dirty and wash indefinitely, and I am not running a laundry. I am not here to assure you that you can go on repeating the same sin until you've had enough. I must confess that the way you've become stubbornly hardened in sin makes it impossible for me to believe in the sincerity of your repentance. On the other side of the grille, the old man began to sob. Hearing him moan and sniffle, Antonia's godfather initially felt nauseous then suddenly gauged how much the man there next to him must be suffering at that very moment, and he was overcome by a wave of pure compassion. This reprobate old man was the neighbor he must love, for the blackness of his suffering soul and not in spite of it; he must love with neither hesitation nor disgust but with all his heart, in the manner of St. Julian the Hospitaller kissing the leper's lips. Antonia reproached him for tolerating evil and, worse still, for not realizing just how bad it was, and he had never been able to persuade her otherwise. She had certainly witnessed things he had never experienced and could no doubt not even imagine—he would grant her that, but she was wrong to think that sin can be quantified like some crime in the Penal Code, in one respect it can be more or less visible, it is always there as a whole, in great crimes as in little ones, equal unto itself, dull, dirty, with neither depth nor nobility, with the result that at the heart of every sin, even the most infinitesimal, the hideous face of the Medusa still grimaces. One must not scream, it's hard, one must not let one's heart turn to stone, which so often he believed was happening to him when he was foundering in the cesspool of the confessional, one must keep watch over living flesh, the stubborn circulation of the blood, because God made man in His own image and in His likeness, and the biblical reference infuriated Antonia, oh, it's not nice to look at, the image and likeness of God, and the model must be even worse, and so he kept to himself any references that sprang to mind, he wondered what she might have seen during her sojourns in the bloody collapse of Yugoslavia whence, in the end, she had not brought back a single photograph, despite the time and money invested in that dream trip of hers, but she refused to say a thing, he could see she was in pain, and, once again, he was responsible for that pain since he was the one who had given her the camera, for her fourteenth birthday, and without it she would never have dreamt of going there in the first place any more than she would have ended up on the Ostriconi road one morning at sunrise in August 2003. *Thou shalt not make unto thee any graven image, or any likeness of any thing that is in heaven above, or that is in the earth beneath, or that is in the water under the earth. Thou shalt not bow down thyself to them, nor serve them.* He had not listened to the Word, and now because of him his goddaughter had served the graven images that had killed her. He did not harbor any tendencies toward iconoclasm, on the contrary: by giving Christ to redeem the world, had God Himself not agreed to hand over His most perfect image? Antonia's godfather likes churches to be filled with statues and paintings, even graceless ones, and he has never felt as if he were serving graven images. In the village, the fourteen stations of the Way of the Cross look as if they have been painted by handicapped children. The unfortunate Simon of Cyrene has been afflicted with one leg dramatically shorter than the other, Saint Veronica is suffering from severe stoutness, and Christ himself is twisted out of shape. It doesn't matter. Images act as a support to one's gaze only so that it will go through them and beyond them to capture the eternal and constantly renewed mystery of the Passion. Yes, images are a door onto eternity. But photography says nothing about eternity, photography revels in the ephemeral, attests to the irreversible, and reflects everything back to the void. If photography had existed in Jesus's time, Christianity would not have developed or, at best, would have been an unspeakable religion of despair. That is when it would have been best to be an iconoclast and let nothing remain. The most realistic pictorial representations of the crucifixion always allow a glimpse within the wounds of martyred flesh, as if in the negative, of the miracle of the Resurrection. If a photograph of the death of Christ could have existed, it would have shown nothing more than a tortured body left to eternal death. In a photograph, even the living are transformed into cadavers because every time the shutter is released, death has already passed by.

O my Father, if it be possible, let this cup pass from me.

But it is not possible, of course. One must seize it and drink. But who handed the cup to Antonia?

He has been silent for far too long, his eyes staring down at the Gospel, raising the hope—soon to be disappointed—among the congregation that he has said his fill. His sister's hands are clenched on the back of the prie-dieu. He has still said nothing about his goddaughter. He starts speaking again, before even deciding to.

Antonia was not, strictly speaking, a good Christian, I know that, and you do, too. While there were times when she could conceive of the existence of God, it was in a very strange way. She did not trust Him, did not place her hopes in Him. In this hour when we are placing her in His hands, we cannot lie, not even to console ourselves, and each of us must feel how ridiculous a lie would be at this time and in this place, in the dwelling of Our Lord, whom it is impossible to deceive. But I also know that Antonia's heart was overflowing with a love that left her particularly vulnerable to pain and, in addition, that pain sometimes leads to rebellion. I know this because I am her uncle and her godfather, because I knew her and loved her, and I ask forgiveness here before you and before God if I do not manage, as I would have liked, to express myself here simply as the priest. I know, finally—above all I know—that God's mercy is infinite and that He penetrates hearts to a depth that is inaccessible to us. Personally, I believe He will welcome Antonia, and that she is already near to Him. However, we are grieving. I have spoken to you of the tears of Christ, awkwardly and at too great a length, and I ask you again to forgive me. Why is he weeping? Because he is torn. We too, are torn. But we must remain torn, must remain there, between hope and grief, both overcome by grief and overflowing with hope. In this way we can believe that Antonia is with the Lord, but we weep for her all the same.

OFFERTORY: *DOMINE JESU CHRISTE*

7
(*Soldier Dying Next to His Doctor*, Corfu, 1915)

L ord Jesus Christ, King of glory, deliver the souls of all the faithful departed from the pains of hell and from the bottomless pit.

In 1901, at the age of sixteen, Rista M. leaves his native town of Šabac to settle in Belgrade. He is probably thinking of becoming a painter, and that is why he initially enrolls in art school. That same year he meets Milan J., a photographer at the court of King Peter, who takes a liking to him and teaches him all the subtle tricks of his art. For there can be no doubt that Rista M. views photography as an art deserving of its *lettres de noblesse*. So he will not become a painter. Nor will he become an artist, even though his work does display an exceptional sense of composition—because one cannot possibly devote one's entire life to beauty when one is born in 1885 in the Balkans.

But of course, in 1901 Rista M. does not know that yet.

He obtains his diploma in 1905 and sets off for Vienna and Berlin. He sends self-portraits to his master, wearing a derby hat and a three-piece suit, his silver watch chain dangling elegantly from a button on his vest. He is clearly happy to be young, impeccably dressed, and exploring Europe. He asks for some money to be sent to him. He arrives in Paris, where he is hired by the Rol Agency. At the Bagatelle Gamefield, he takes pictures of aviators' exploits, princely weddings, bicycle races, state funerals; he sets his camera up in cathedrals and at race tracks, he seems to be specializing in society events, but he has not forgotten that photography is an art, and he is still arbitrating with the same virtuosity between emptiness and fullness, shadow and light.

In September 1907, the *Herald Tribune* takes him on as a correspondent, after awarding him a prize for one of his photographs. The image depicts a greyhound belonging to Gabriele d'Annunzio finishing the race in the lead a few inches from the Comtesse de Noailles's hound. The two dogs are running side-by-side, their paws do not touch the ground, every muscle in their long bodies is strained beneath their dark coats as they burst into the frame from the right, from a point located somewhere above. One must study the image carefully to see that this is not a somewhat academic, classical painting, but a photograph whose composition must have been determined in a fraction of a second. Certain details in the shadows may have been enhanced with charcoal, unless a perfect exposure made any touch-ups unnecessary.

One might conjecture—altogether pointlessly—that if the history of Europe had turned out differently, Rista M. would have become a famous photographer. After growing weary of traveling and assiduously seeking out the aristocracy, he would eventually—once he had saved enough money—have devoted himself to fine-art photography.

But in 1912, a few months after Gaston C. returned from Tripolitania, Dragutin D., known as Apis, head of intelligence for the general staff, summons Rista M. to Belgrade. Apis is not only a passionate conspirator and a regicide, who has preserved the memory of the assassination of King Alexander I of Serbia and his wife Draga in the form not of vague mental images but of three bullets still lodged in his own body; he is also a man who has understood the role photography can play in war propaganda. Henceforth, Rista M. will no longer be chronicling society events. He follows the Serbian Army, their standards blessed by the patriarch, onto victorious fields of battle all the way to Macedonia, where the Turks have just been driven out. In Skopje, a delegation consisting of the city's religious authorities is expecting King Peter. As captured by Rista's camera lens, two priests—one Orthodox, the other Roman Catholic—a rabbi, and an imam are walking abreast to meet the king. Alexander, the heir to the throne, will also be arriving in Skopje before long. While waiting, Rista M. walks around town with his camera. Hussars strapped into short jackets with frog fasteners, a long white plume quivering on their bearskin busbies, are riding through the streets. In a doorway, three Serbian foot soldiers, their rifles on their shoulders, are smoking a cigarette, and behind them, very nearly overexposed but not quite, one can make out the white dome and minaret of a mosque.

Rista M. has not lost any of his sense of composition.

As the Second Balkan War is beginning, he takes a picture of men squatting in a circle in a clearing around an old soldier in a fez telling a story. They look like a group of enthralled children. In the background, between two trees and outlined against the sun, an officer stands watching them, or perhaps also trying to listen to the old man.

No, Rista M. has lost none of his sense of composition.

In July 1913, he goes back to Paris, in all likelihood quite gladly. If he has the opportunity to see the wonderful color photographs, taken that same year on an English beach in Dorset, of a young girl dressed in red, he will not fail to marvel at them. When it comes to delicacy and beauty, photography can hold its own against painting. The young girl, the boat on the pebbles, the white cliffs and the sea are all snatched from the race of time, set beyond its reach in a place that will forever preserve the soft texture of the girl's skin, the integrity of hallowed flesh, youth.

Perhaps, at the time, Rista M. is nurturing the illusion that the short hiatus war had introduced in his life has just ended for good. He stops believing this when Gavrilo P., despite the unbelievable amateurism of his preparations, miraculously manages to shoot Franz Ferdinand: the archduke, blinded by the deceptive powers of destiny, had been struggling all day long to catch up with his elusive death in the streets of Sarajevo. The conspirators are fished out of the Miljacka, arrested on the street. They vomit bile and old, ineffective cyanide onto the uniforms of the policemen who have surrounded them.

Rista M. rushes back to Serbia. He now knows that the worst is yet to come. He is afraid he might never see his family again. He returns to Šabac to embrace them but arrives too late, finding only his mother. All his brothers have already been mobilized. His mind is no longer on famous athletes, or princesses led to the altar in virginal white dresses, or the delicate, noble curve of a greyhound's spine. In Belgrade, he traipses from office to office to obtain permission to go to the front as a photographer because he is convinced that only in that way can he be useful. He is given his press pass. He takes pictures of everything—the enthusiasm of mobilization, the columns of refugees, two horsemen riding nonchalantly past a Hungarian corpse half melted in the mud, Šabac in ruins, its church burned, the battle at Cer, the battle at the Kolubara river, which the Serbian troops ford on makeshift bridges, the typhus victims. Perhaps he crosses paths with John R., who has been sent away from the Western front because in a moment of enthusiasm, to try out the brand-new Luger PO8 that an affable German officer had lent him, he fired in the direction of the French trenches; now he is wandering every which way through the Balkans, from Salonika to Belgrade, from battlefield to cabaret, in the company of a Canadian artist, drunk like him on war and *rakija*.

The army has entrusted Rista M. with the task of developing any rolls of film he might find on Austrian soldiers. The first thing the developer reveals is peasant women tied to a pole, the tips of their toes dangling a foot from the ground, yet they seem to be trying still, in vain, to find a foothold; then comes a forest of gallows around which the Austrians are calmly conversing, smiles on their lips. Rista M. discovers that, oddly enough, men like to keep a touching memory of their crimes, as they might of their wedding, or the birth of their children, or any other signif-icant moment in their life, with the same innocence. The inven-tion of photography has afforded them the irresistible opportu-nity to indulge in this penchant. The thought that they might actually be testifying against themselves in the most devastating way apparently does not occur to them. Why should they care? All through the century that is just beginning, they will take pic-tures of their victims—gunned down, hanged, or crucified along a road in Anatolia, as if in an interplay of mirrors multiplying Christ's image to infinity—they themselves will pose, tirelessly, at the edge of a pit full of naked bodies in Byelorussia, in front of a row of severed heads in the Congo, or, at the camp at Jasenovac, next to a prisoner whose neck they are about to saw through. They would pose in the same way in front of a famous monument, a hunting trophy, or simply at the end of a good meal among friends. The era, the clothing might change, but the faces still express the same feeling—not quite joy but something lighter, more futile: nonchalance, a carefree well-being.

By the end of 1914, Rista M. is keeping a record of casual horror.

He accumulates photographs of torture, classifies them, annotates them. In 1916, they are exhibited at the Louvre and at the Victoria and Albert Museum before being sent to the United States. The bestiality of the enemy has now been docu-mented, and everyone can gorge on the spectacle while grant-ing themselves the luxury of indignation. There is talk of hold-ing a parallel exhibition somewhere between Budapest and Berlin.

In October 1915, Bulgaria enters the war. A few weeks later, caught in a pincer movement, Serbia crumbles. The army, the government, the Regent Alexander, old King Peter, lying in a cart pulled by oxen, Rista M., his camera, and a troop of famished refugees begin a long retreat in the depths of winter that will lead them over the Albanian mountains to the Adriatic coast. They make their way through the snow, ford the frozen waters of the Drin, the soldiers use their rifles as crutches, and every day the column litters the path of its dying hours with corpses.

For the first time, Rista M. neglects his composition.

Everything is white. It is impossible to distinguish foreground from background, which would give an illusion of depth. A frozen sentry has collapsed in a world become two-dimensional.

A small boy wrapped in layers of rags trains on the lens the sickly clarity of his fascinated blue eyes.

A soldier leans against a tree and stares at the absence of horizon.

Rista M. continues to advance. He takes pictures of hunger, fever, the resigned men who have left the column to sit off in the snow in a movement of weariness and relief. He arrives at last in Shëngjin where the French Navy is assembling survivors to ferry them to Corfu. Makeshift hospitals have been set up in tents: Rista M. tours them. A dazed doctor is sitting next to a naked man so thin he seems to have been stripped of flesh. Every detail of his skeleton is visible, as if he were a plate out of a medical encyclopedia. His stomach has disappeared from beneath his rib cage, and one could swear that his internal organs have disappeared, too. The circumference of his thigh is no greater than that of his femur. Enormous kneecaps have distended the skin on his knees. The tip of his hip bone is sticking out at the bottom of his back. But his face remains astonishingly human, filled with melancholy resignation. Rista

M. presses the shutter. He does not try to find the best angle. He simply wants to keep a trace of what is happening here. On the back of the photograph, he will write: *Died fifteen minutes later.*

As the days go by, Rista M. regains his sense of composition. No doubt his health has improved, he is eating his fill, has started to enjoy harmony again, and the horizon is newly visible.

In the distance, battleships are dropping anchor. In the foreground, a small boat is leaving the dock to head out to sea, with a man standing in the bow, his hands on his hips as he turns to face the photographer. In the stern, a second man, seen from behind, is holding an oar. The boat is overflowing with a twisted tangle of corpses. There are too many bodies to bury, so the blue waters of the Mediterranean will be their cemetery. Lines added in charcoal emphasize the movement of the waves, the shadows, the ships' hulls. Rista M. is again giving a nod to painting. He knows how to bring out the timeless content of the moment. The two men have become boatmen across the river Styx, and it is easy to imagine that in every mouth of every body they are ferrying is a silver obol.

Deliver them from the lion's mouth
That hell swallow them not up
That they fall not into darkness.

At the end of the war, Rista M. settles in Belgrade. His country has changed its name, as it will do again on numerous occasions. It is now Peter I, King of the Serbs, Croats, and Slovenes, by the grace of God and the will of his people, who delivers a passport printed in French and Serbo-Croatian to M., Rista, thirty-four years of age, journalist, average height, long face, light brown hair, blue eyes, regular nose, regular mouth and mustache, who in 1929 will become the subject of

Alexander I, King of Yugoslavia. He works for the press service of the Ministry of Foreign Affairs before founding his own agency. He takes pictures of the royal family, of the princesses playing with their dolls, of the heir to the throne, of King Alexander riding on horseback into the dappled light of forest undergrowth. He experiments with color, with the movement of life in the parks and streets of Belgrade.

In 1930, he is present at the inauguration of a monument on whose pedestal these words are carved: *Aimons la France comme elle nous a aimés.*[3]

In 1934, now that he knows that hiatuses never really end, he covers Hermann Göring's visit to Belgrade. He does, however, continue to take impeccably composed pictures of daily life and domestic bliss. Does he see something there besides a long procession of shadows and ghosts? In any case, he does not seem to be interested in anything else. He does not accompany Alexander to France. He does not hear the shots, the horses whinnying, the screams of the crowd when panicked policemen begin emptying their weapons. There are many photographers watching the king—whose portrait Rista M. has taken so often—as the blood oozes from his body, there, inside the official car, now stopped on the Canebière, but Rista M. is not among them.

He hears that civil war has just broken out in Spain.

One year later, while Rista M. is following couples strolling along the banks of the river Sava, a petty NKVD bureaucrat at the Lubyanka, who no doubt has never looked on photography as an art, is recording through his camera lens a daily procession of all those who know they are destined to die or be deported to Kolyma. He then painstakingly files away all their portraits, on which he has written their names, patronymic, and surnames. Z., Aleksey Ivanovich; B., Anna Moiiseyevna; B., Evgenia

---

[3] Let us love France as she has loved us. (T.N.)

Yuzefovna; V., Elizaveta Alekseyevna; M., Osip Emilyevich; V., Vladimir Nilovich; they are forty, sixteen, twenty, or seventy-two years of age, they are poets or illiterates, carpenters, workers, pensioners, Orthodox priests, translators. In their eyes, one can read anger, irony, terror, defiance, despondency, or astonishment, but the diversity of their individual reactions matters little because, in carrying out his fastidious administrative task, the NKVD employee has unwittingly made the presence of death tangible, death that has settled inside every one of them and against which they do not even think of struggling. They are all confronting the same thing, which is neither the camera, nor the employee holding it (who will, in all likelihood, soon take their place), but an indescribable face whose monstrous features have already petrified their hearts. In their silence of stone, it is as if they are all reciting the same words, words written in a notebook in big hesitant capital letters by little Mark Salomonovich N. at the time of his parents' arrest: *Mama Papa Lyuka Izya we're dead all of us that's how it is.*

Let the standard-bearer holy Michael lead them into that holy light.

That's how it is. One must forget the images of life, leave behind the languid lovers of Kalemegdan Park. Now there is another war, the fourth to take Rista M. with it. On March 27, 1941, he joins the demonstration against a treaty that the Regent Paul has just signed with the Axis. The regent flees. On April 6, the Germans launch Operation Retribution. Rista M. runs through Belgrade under the bombs, taking pictures of death's return, gutted buildings, tramway lines crumpled like paper toys, bodies lying along Knez Mihailova. When Milan N. becomes prime minister of the Government of National Salvation, Rista M. resigns. He goes on taking photographs in secret. He becomes a wanted man. He goes underground. In

1943, he escapes from three men who are pursuing him by hiding in a house. He cannot resist taking their picture through the window. He waits for the three men to be properly positioned in the frame, neither too close nor too far away from each other, and when one of them suddenly turns to one side, creating an interesting break in symmetry, Rista presses the shutter. On the back of his personal print, he writes: *Collaborators searching for the author of this photo to kill him.*

At the same time in Zagreb, Curzio M. is being received by the leader of the Independent State of Croatia who, full of emotion, is showing him the precious gift his Ustaše have brought him, a salad bowl filled with gouged-out eyeballs. While it may not be wise to take Curzio M.'s testimony too literally, one can only admire the talent he displays in condensing the multiplicity of complex situations into a single unforgettable parable.

In April 1944, it is the turn of the Allied forces to drop their bombs.

In October, the Red Army enters Belgrade. Rista M. captures scenes of jubilation, laughter, and bouquets of flowers, and his son running next to an enormous JS-2 tank, in and out of the Soviet soldiers' legs. But he knows that the joy of a crowd can only truly be complete if there is blood, and because he is a photographer and his profession demands that he keep a trace of everything that ever happened here, he also takes pictures of lynchings and summary executions. A partisan spots him, runs over, smashes his camera. They confiscate all his controversial photographs. The only images he manages to rescue of Belgrade's liberation are the flowers, the women's smiles, the affable, brotherly faces of the Red Army soldiers, and his son running next to a tank.

He starts up his agency again in the new Federal People's Republic of Yugoslavia. He offers no classes in painting or drawing, but rather in photojournalism.

In 1955, when he turns seventy, he retires.

When he dies in April 1969, the United States is at war in Vietnam, and Rista M. has not taken a single photo in nine years. We do not know the reason for his sudden and total abdication. Age is not the likely cause. Perhaps Rista M. has ended up feeling disgusted by those images that will never be the equal of a painting because, in the end, it is not as an art that photography shows the true measure of its power. Its domain is not that of eternal beauty. It slices into the flow of time like implacable Fate, and that is something it alone has the power to do. If that is indeed the case, by the time Rista M. was an old man he must have realized that his whole life long he had been led astray, down a path that was not his.

But perhaps he simply stopped because in his opinion there were no pictures left to take in the worn-out world around him. Everything had been said, repeated ad nauseam in an unbearable stammer. It is even quite possible that on the threshold of death he was sorry he had not stopped much earlier, in Corfu, at the end of the month of December 1915. Because in 1969, he can no longer ignore the fact that on that day, in a tent in a field hospital, at the edge of the blue graveyard of the Mediterranean, he not only took the picture of an emaciated, dying soldier, he also captured, once and for all, in a single striking image, the face of the century.

Which Thou didst promise of old to Abraham and to his seed.

SANCTUS

8
(*East German Border Guards Creating a Breach in the Wall,*
Berlin, 1989)

When in March 1989 Pascal B. was arrested for the third time, Antonia did not run to cry on her uncle's shoulder. She knew at once that she would not be able to put up with the waiting, or with other people's self-indulgent gazes of compassion. She also knew she was trapped in an endless cycle that would never let her go, as if she were orbiting an incredibly vast planet. The life that lay ahead would merely repeat everything that had gone before. Pascal B. would be sent to jail, then get out of jail, then be sent again, over and over, and she would be there waiting, getting older and older and ever more disillusioned, until it was too late. On her tombstone they wouldn't carve her name but, more soberly, "Pascal B.'s woman," and that would only be fair because the center of gravity of her entire existence would have always been situated somewhere outside of herself. Obviously, to complain about her lover's selfishness was taboo. How could you accuse someone who was willing to sacrifice his life and liberty to a political cause of being selfish? There would be nothing she could do but enjoy Pascal B.'s presence during those spells of freedom. But that very presence itself was totally intermittent, especially since Antonia had been living in Ajaccio. She saw him two or three times a week, she never knew when, he only notified her at the last minute, he sometimes called before showing up at her place in the middle of the night, and she often picked up a suspicious whiff of female perfume on his skin. The fact that

Pascal B. belonged to an underground organization gave him a few practical advantages. He was never supposed to say where he was, or what he was doing, or who he was with, and there was little doubt that he used this imperative of professional secrecy to indulge in activities that had very little to do with French colonialism or the struggle for national liberation. She did not hold it against him. She knew him, the way she knew all the boys she had grown up with, for whom the female sex could be divided quite simply into two categories that were not only distinct but also inalterably impermeable: a woman was either respectable, or she was not. A man's official companion obviously belonged to the first category, where she was in the company of mothers, aunts, and sisters. Any other representative of the female sex belonged to the second category, among whom the men were at leisure to take an occasional lover without any repercussions. And while it was considered advisable to hide these brief adulterous affairs, it was not out of a sense of remorse, or even in acknowledgement of the faintest moral significance, but in order to spare the legitimate wife or companion, who was not expected to understand, let alone validate, such a subtly dichotomous view of the world. More trivially, it made it possible to avoid a fair amount of hassle. Antonia knew all this only too well because she had accepted it long ago. She did not really feel jealous, just annoyed at the naïveté of his perpetual secretive existence, and faintly disgusted, as if she were being forced to sleep in a fug of unclean sheets.

She didn't write to Pascal B., she didn't send him any pictures. She requested a visitor's permit, which she obtained after a few weeks. For the first time in her life, she was entering a prison. She followed the guard into the filth of long yellow corridors, and every clanging of a lock made her jump. Pascal B. was waiting for her in the visiting room. He was smiling. He didn't complain about the absence of letters. She was happy to see him, even in this vile place, and she was afraid she might not be able to speak to him the way she had planned. He took her hand.

They don't have anything on me, you know. It'll end up being dismissed again, don't worry. I'll get out.

Sure you will, she said. You'll get out. But how soon?

He shrugged.

A few months, a year, I don't know. They're in no hurry, you know, the investigating magistrates.

She leaned toward him and said gently, Pascal. I'm not going to wait for you. This time, I'm not going to wait for you.

He stiffened in his chair.

You came here to tell me this? Here?

Yes, I came here to tell you this. Would you have rather I'd have written?

He looked down without answering. She gathered up all her courage and added that she still loved him, but she didn't want any more of this life, and she knew there was no point in asking him to give up the life he'd chosen, and even if there was any point, she wouldn't ask him, she didn't want him to give up anything for her sake, he'd only end up holding it against her, but if she went on like this, she would hold it against him, to be honest, she already did, because of the life he was imposing on her even if he didn't mean to, she didn't want such a life, and she couldn't wait until he got out to tell him, she couldn't go on putting on an act for months or an entire year or even longer, so she had decided it was better to come and tell him right away.

He looked up at her.

I'm going back to my cell, he murmured, and he called for the guard.

She kept hold of his hand while he slowly got up from his chair, Pascal, wait a minute, she was speaking quickly, I'm not strong, I can't stand this, but I'm not abandoning you, I'll never abandon you, I'll always be there for you, you'll see, I'm not abandoning you, you have to know that, you can count on me even more than if I—but he was standing across from her now. He didn't want to listen to her anymore. I'm going back to my cell. He turned his back and followed the guard. She hated seeing him suffer because of her. She hated even more the effort she was making in spite of herself to ease her conscience. She went back to Corsica burdened with the weight of a misdeed she refused to lighten.

When Madeleine O. heard about their breakup, she went to the trouble of driving all the way to Ajaccio to see Antonia at the agency.

It's disgusting, what you did. Don't even think about ever speaking to me again.

Madeleine was addressing her in a tone of outraged virtue, as if her own behavior had always been irreproachable and under no circumstances could challenge the legitimacy of her moral authority. This left Antonia more admiring than hurt.

Very funny, Madeleine, she replied, but I really don't have time for a laugh, I have a lot of work. Get the hell out of here.

The following Saturday, she spent two days in the village with her parents. Her godfather tried to hide his relief when he found out she was free of Pascal B. at last. He was smart or tactful enough to know that Antonia would not appreciate it if he were to display any pleasure or, worse still, criticize the jilted lover. He showed her renewed affection and left it at that.

He was the only one.

As she sat on the terrace of the bar over a cup of coffee she'd allowed to go cold, she felt as if she'd become a ghost, haunting a house to the complete indifference of its inhabitants. Not one of her friends said hello. No one even went so far as to meet her gaze. She could have got up and left. Pride kept her sitting there. She did not have to justify herself to anyone, let alone feel ashamed. At the end of the afternoon, Simon

T. showed up. She expected him to walk right by her as if he hadn't seen her, but he kissed her on the cheek and sat down next to her. From inside the bar, Jean-Joseph C. shot him a look of reproach that Simon met without flinching before starting up a friendly conversation with Antonia. When she got up to go back to her parents', she put one hand on his shoulder and said thank you. He gave a tremor and murmured something totally unintelligible. Only then did she realize that Simon's feelings toward her were not purely friendly. The boy was in love with her, and she really must be blind, stupid, or supremely indifferent not to have noticed earlier what he was hiding so awkwardly, for he must have been in love with her for a very long time, maybe not since the time they danced that parody of a tango together at the village feast, but for a long time all the same, that was why he was so sensitive to everything she said to him, and so easily hurt, that was why he had been unable to resist the ridiculous temptation to make himself known to her in the van, not because he was a braggart—like most of the FLNC militants she knew, who could not help but share with any willing listener, particularly a perfect stranger, their tales of exploits they had probably not even committed, with the result that their uninterrupted deluge of spontaneous confessions must have complicated the job of the police much more than any hypothetical *omertà* would have done—but because he was in love, in love and desperate, because he knew that most of the girls were always promised to older boys with whom it was all the more inconceivable for him to compete given that he admired them beyond all bounds, Pascal B. to start with, whom he admired even more than the others, virtually to the point of worshipping him, which left him no other choice than to wallow miserably in the secrecy of his impossible love, with no hope of ever confessing it one day, particularly as Antonia, in breaking up with Pascal B. during his detention, had rendered the taboo weighing over her even more absolute, leaving her inaccessible once and for all. Antonia suspected that, far from creating a barrier to the troublesome love he bore her, her inaccessibility was its main cause, perhaps its only cause. It was not Antonia herself Simon loved, but "Pascal B.'s woman"—in other words, basically, Pascal B. himself. None of this was particularly flattering. At least she need not fear Simon would be forward and force her into a difficult confrontation that would jeopardize her relationship with the only person who did not treat her like a leper.

Two weeks later, she received an extraordinary letter from Pascal B. He understood her, he understood her very well, even if, naturally, it wasn't easy for him to give her up. All those years must have been really hard on her, even if he had never gone to the trouble of thinking about them, something he would like to apologize for, and she had every right to want a different future, he'd been angry with her, but that was over now, he had nothing to reproach her with, in fact he'd never had anything to reproach her with, and, above all, he trusted her, he knew he could go on counting on her, despite their parting, more than on anyone else, and when he thought about this, he was almost happy, and he was eager to get out of there and see her again. This time, Antonia had to hold back her tears of love and gratitude. Pascal B. was the only one who could relieve her of the burden she was carrying, and she had never imagined he would do it. He had such a huge, good heart, rather rough and modest, to be sure, but huge. His fits of anger never lasted long, she should have known that. In 1979, when he'd beaten up the tourist who spilled his coffee, the very next day he went back into town on his own to look for his victim and apologize. He never confessed this to anyone, not even his closest friends, who had a lot of trouble telling goodness from weakness, and he waited years to tell Antonia alone how he'd gone all over town, every which way, all afternoon, scouring the beaches and ice cream parlors and all the places those useless tourists generally liked to hang out, but in vain because the guy could not be found, perhaps he was hiding at the far end of his campsite and wouldn't come out again until his vacation was ending, and Pascal B. was about to give up when he spotted him leaving the sailing school, and he called out to him, waving and running toward him, which was clearly not a good idea because the other guy, misinterpreting the meaning of this commendable urge to repent, also set off at a run at once at such a breakneck pace that it was impossible to catch up with him. To be sure, Pascal B. had a fiery temperament, and as soon as he caught his breath he railed against the tourist whose ingratitude had prevented him from making amends and who could, therefore, to use the words that Antonia recalled only too well, bloody go and fuck himself. In spite of its disappointing conclusion, this episode spoke volumes about Pascal B.'s huge, good heart.

Antonia was sorry she had split up with him. She very nearly wrote back to tell him she'd been out of her mind, that she wanted to be with him after all. She let herself drift, helpless, in a space that was dangerously close to the great distant planet, at the extreme limit of her gravitational field. She imagined Pascal's return, the warmth of their embrace, the morning of their first awakening when she would sense his presence there next to her in the rumpled bed. She lingered on this image, right down to every specific detail, until their very specificity was enough to break the spell of the lie. She would open her eyes, he would be there, but once the intoxication of their reunion had worn off, on that first morning, she would realize that she had just slipped back into the trap it had been so hard to get out of, and that it was all about to start again, not the way she'd imagined, but exactly the way it had always been, with the same implacable, toxic, and terribly real apathy. She would make him his coffee, then she would suddenly be projected into the past and immersed in shifting sands of anxiety. That mustn't happen. It mustn't. When she saw him again, she would have to resist, beware of her own self, not count on some fluctuating lucidity. No, clearly, she couldn't trust herself. Her firmest resolutions would never be any more solid than the versatile inconsistency of thought. Something more was needed, but she didn't know what.

That very evening, at a piano bar in the port where she'd gone with colleagues from the newspaper, she yielded to the advances of a guy who had never heard of Pascal B. He took her back to his place. She was curious to touch, at long last, another man's skin. It was fairly disappointing. As she was getting dressed, he asked her to stay, to spend the night with him. No way, she replied. When she went back to her village two weeks later, everyone said hello, reticently. Pascal B. had obviously sent orders from prison that no one dared to defy. Madeleine, together with Laetitia, sought her out on the terrace of the bar, looking sheepish.

Listen, Antonia, I'm really, you know—

Antonia, magnanimous, spared her the humiliation of apologizing.

Let's talk about something else. Have a seat.

They sat down, but no one spoke. Antonia was smiling, even though something had been broken for good. In a way she pitied Madeleine for feeling things only in order to conform or to obey an order, but above all she despised her with all her heart. It didn't matter. After all, you didn't choose your friends any more than you chose your family. Simon showed up, euphoric about the general reconciliation, and the atmosphere relaxed slightly. They ordered drinks. Madeleine and Laetitia became quite affectionate again, and their sincerity was all the more pathetic in that it could not be questioned. Antonia would have had greater respect for their hypocrisy. Simon told them he had to go to Ajaccio in a few days and casually suggested to Antonia that maybe they could meet up for a drink.

She studied him with a certain interest.

At that very moment, the solution to her problem came to her. Not some vague thought, but a simple, unforgivable, definitive act. She had to sleep with Simon. Once would be enough. If she pulled it off, she would raise an insurmountable wall between herself and Pascal B. She wouldn't even need to tell him, which would only incur the risk of hurting him terribly and seeing him disappear completely from her life, something she feared more than anything; it would be enough for her to know what she had done for her to resist, no matter the power of temptation, in fact she wouldn't even have to resist: any going back would become objectively impossible. And, naturally, Simon would not say anything either. All that remained was to convince the interested party—something which, in Antonia's opinion, should not be that difficult, as the outcome of a conflict between loyalty and desire rarely left any doubt.

Good idea. Call me when you're in Ajaccio, she said to Simon.

And of course he called her. They had dinner together, and Antonia took him to a nightclub where there was little risk of running into nationalist militants in search of rumors to peddle. At three o'clock in the morning, Simon saw her back to her door.

Would you like to come up for a drink?

He looked stunned.

What?

Would you like to come up for a drink? she said again.

I'd rather not, he said.

Why? Where's the harm in it? We're friends, aren't we?

He nodded, showing every sign of extreme embarrassment. She took him by the arm.

So, if we're friends, come up for a drink, I'm not sleepy, and I don't want to drink all on my own.

Maybe, as they went up the stairs, Simon managed to convince himself that she was telling the truth, that she simply wanted to have a drink with a friend and she was not deliberately putting him in a position where he might do something loathsome, but as soon as they went through the door, she proved him wrong by throwing herself into his arms. He shoved her away with a horrified spontaneity that offended her deeply. And so there were times when loyalty turned out to be stronger than desire. This almost never happens, thought Antonia, it's common knowledge, but it would have to happen to me, because I'm Pascal B.'s woman, it was because of Pascal B. that she was desired, and it was also because of Pascal B. that she was rejected, she felt humiliated and angry, her plan completely slipped her mind, she was forgetting that if it were not for Pascal B. in the first place she would never have invited Simon up, and for the first time in her life it was with a sort of hatred that she thought about that man who had taken up and was still taking up all the space in her life to such a degree as to make her invisible, why? she asked Simon—why? Don't you want to? and as she asked him she realized how much she herself wanted to, but Simon was recoiling toward the door, trembling, shaking his head, of course I want to, but I can't do that, my God, you know very well I can't, why not? Antonia cried, she grabbed him by the shoulders, ran her hands up his neck to his face, I've had too much to drink, she thought, but she wanted him to look at her, she wanted all the shadows Pascal B. was projecting into the room to fade away, so that Simon would see her, and her alone, that was all she wanted, and in the end he did see her. The next morning when she woke up, Simon was lying next to her in a fetal position, sobbing like a child. She tried to comfort him, held him close, covered him with kisses, his forehead, his shoulders, his cheeks. She wanted to appear chaste and compassionate, but she was still trembling with the unfamiliar pleasure that in the night had possessed her body and soul, and the more she kissed Simon, the more turbulent her kisses became, deep, insistent. She turned him over on his back and sat astride him, and when he closed his arms around her, his eyes were still moist, but he had stopped weeping. They stayed in bed all morning. Simon went to take a shower. When he came out of the bathroom, Antonia, completely naked, was lighting incense and a candle. He found her very beautiful. She smiled at him above the flame as it flickered in a graceful dance, as today a candle flame is dancing, although it is illuminating no smiles. No matter how intently Simon stares at that flame, Antonia's face does not appear. Her heart was not overflowing with love. It's not true, even if her godfather is doing his utmost to believe it. In any case it was not overflowing with love for Simon. Ever since that night they spent together in April 1989, she'd never stopped treating him more or less like shit. He went back to the village in a trance that day, pure bliss mingling with the sorrow of unbearable remorse. He was crushed by his betrayal, it was too much for him, so much that even love could not redeem it. But love could at least provide an explanation, because it really was about love, and he was sure he would see Antonia again soon. He waited for her to call, and she didn't. When he could wait no more and picked up the phone, she answered, her tone cheery, as if nothing had happened. He felt as if he were tipping into an abyss. There was no love, not the slightest trace. He had betrayed everything that was dearest to him for something that was nothing more than a banal sexual encounter. The thought of it was unbearable. He could not look himself in the mirror. He would wake up in the middle of the night, biting his fists. He stopped calling her. He ran into her in the village. She did not even do him the honor of seeming uncomfortable around him. He could have believed he'd dreamt it all, and had it been possible, he would have believed it and been infinitely relieved. In June, she asked him to come and see her in Ajaccio. He thought she was going to explain everything, but her explanation consisted once again in throwing her arms around him with so much passion that once again he yielded. I've been thinking about you all the time, she said, if you only knew, and she undressed him, kept him from sleeping, then put her hands on his face, and he could feel the soft tips of her fingers gently stroking his eyelids. Then, not a word from her all summer. It was incomprehensible. Until she called him again at the end of September. Inner tensions were rocking the nationalist movement, leading to a first split. Simon spent all his time at political meetings. He went to see her all the same. This time he asked her: why are you doing this to me? She seemed truly sorry. You know I love you dearly, Simon, you know that, at least? No, he didn't. His mother—when Antonia's godfather abandoned her like a sick dog to enter the service of a God that does not even exist—must not have understood either what the members of this family meant, exactly, by the word "love," even when it was qualified by an adverb. I wish none of this had happened, he said to her, but it wasn't true, even today it's not true, in spite of the pain, the waste, in spite of the betrayal and the fear of being found out, and he can see himself as he was, trembling like a leaf on his way to greet Pascal B., newly released from prison in 1990, just before the final explosion of the movement to which he had devoted his life, he sees himself anxiously studying Pascal's face, Pascal who is smiling and hugging him, oh, Simon my man! he can see himself throwing up by the side of the road, and he can see himself, less than two weeks later, his face buried between Antonia's thighs with the same desperate avidity as Judas receiving thirty miserable pieces of silver, about to scatter them at the foot of the tree where he will hang himself. Simon did not hang himself. His betrayal went on burning like an ulcer. And then one day in 1991, after months of meetings that went nowhere, of friendships transformed into inextinguishable hatred, of enraged militants standing on their chairs exchanging insults and death threats, while Antonia was taking pictures of the war in Yugoslavia, Pascal B. said to Simon, this will not end well, it's going to be terrible, and we're going to have to live through it together. He was staring into space. Something else we'll have to share. But we've already shared a lot, haven't we? And then his gaze met Simon's long enough for there to be no more ambiguity regarding what he was referring to, his gaze bored right into Simon's heart, and it liquefied as Pascal's stone face lit up with a smile. He had found out, God knows how, and Simon had just received the most elegant of absolutions, to which the only response was silence. Oh, Simon, murmured Pascal, finally looking away. Antonia went on calling him, after long periods of silence, with no explanation, no thought for his feelings. When in 1993 she informed him she would be having an abortion, he protested, he was not okay with it, they had to talk, but she replied that it was no concern of his, in any way, and he told her that for him she had ceased to exist and he didn't want to see her anymore. But of course he saw her again. He eased into her as if into the waters of the resurrection. If she hadn't died, he would never have stopped seeing her. Without ever understanding. In November 1989, he was still at her place. The first split had taken place one month earlier, and at the time no one knew it would lead to a second one. He was complaining about it to Antonia. She stood up, naked, lit by candlelight, and as always it took his breath away. Wait, she said. She rummaged in a drawer and came to sit cross-legged next to him.

I've been doing this for a month. These are the pictures of the general assembly where the new movement was created. You see, I was there.

Simon looked at the pictures and recognized his former friends. She handed him yet another.

This is Berlin, one week ago.

A section of wall has been cut away and pushed forward. Through the breach, three young border guards are visible, standing tall and straight on the East German side. Gérard M.'s photograph was taken from the West, where a huge crowd is milling, dozens of cameras and flashguns in their midst. The young border guards are terribly alone behind the crumbling section of wall. They do not seem happy, just stunned and incredulous.

You see, Simon?

Simon nodded.

This is what is happening in the world right now. Away from your little schoolyard squabbles, I mean. This picture, obviously, you know I didn't take it. I take pictures of fucking stupid general assemblies in crap village halls with fifty guys founding a political party no one gives a shit about and they call it historic.

Once again, she was behaving cruelly toward him, but perhaps above all toward herself. It was the first time she had spoken to him about a subject that meant a lot to her, even though Simon did not know that. He just remembers how she waved the picture in his face, and she was naked, and the candle was burning on the night table. He remembers that she was alive. If he held out his hand, he would feel her flesh and not the coffin. Of all the texts in the funeral mass, the *Sanctus* is the only one where the words do not change because it is not about human beings, where they were born and where they died, but only about the Lord, the Lord God of Hosts. *Heaven and earth are full of Thy glory*—fingertips caressing eyelids, the soft flesh of the index finger. Simon watches the candle flame dancing, and he is still looking out for Antonia's smile, and he closes his eyes. In the mass they are singing today, as elaborated over the centuries in a tiny village in the heart of Corsica, it is not only the words of the *Sanctus* that are unchanging but also its melody, so when one listens with one's eyes closed, it is impossible to know whether the service one is attending is for the living or the departed.

PATER NOSTER

9
(FLNC Press Conference, Tavera, 1990)

I n August 1990, while Iraqi troops were invading Kuwait, and Yugoslavia had already begun its slow, bloody disintegration, Antonia went to the site of an attack thirty miles south of Ajaccio. A holiday resort had been bombed, but some of the devices had not gone off and a few buildings remained intact. One of them was still covered with the warnings the FLNC commandos had scrawled in huge capital letters to inform any careless passersby of the imminent danger of explosion. On one wall, a militant in a playful mood had gone to the trouble of illustrating the clandestine organization's initials with a large childish flower and a round bomb surmounted with a smoking fuse. Just below it he had written, proving he had no more of a gift for spelling than for the visual arts, DANJER MINED! The charitable hypothesis of a single careless mistake was, unfortunately, not admissible, because the same warning could be seen in several places, with the same ridiculous spelling. Antonia took a picture of the wall with its embellishment and the pile of rubble in the background.

On the following day, her photograph was on the front page of the newspaper.

Several hours after it appeared, Antonia received a call from Pascal B.

I have to see you. I'm at the bar just downstairs, I'll wait for you.

No sooner had she joined him than he began to air his grievances. He suspected her of being deliberately malicious.

Was there nothing else to shoot? Did she realize that she made them look not only like a bunch of half-wits but illiterate as well?

I don't know if the guy who wrote that is a half-wit, but one thing is for sure, he's illiterate, and that's not my fault.

She added that the leader of the commando, whoever he was, had not shown much foresight in entrusting a task involving writing, no matter how basic, to the illiterate in question.

The walls were not supposed to remain standing! Pascal protested. How am I supposed to keep track of things like that? Besides, normally any old idiot can handle a can of spray paint, don't you think? What are we, supposed to start screening them?

And the flower? Antonia asked.

I didn't notice, conceded Pascal. I had other things to think about. Besides, I'll say it again, there should've been no more wall. But believe me, that shit-eater Xavier heard me.

Antonia burst out laughing. Pascal wasn't laughing. It wasn't funny. She didn't realize. The atmosphere was dreadful. They were headed toward a major split, even more serious than the last one. God knew how it would finish. Of course, everything was the fault of the other side, a gang of deceitful, cowardly stool pigeons, they'd do anything, and at that very moment, they were probably dining out on the unexpected gift Antonia had just presented to them—all the more so, Pascal added, in that normally they were the half-wits! Oh, what an ass that Xavier was! I should have given him a good hiding while I was at it!

Pascal looked exhausted. There were deep shadows beneath his bloodshot eyes. Antonia felt sorry for him. Nothing he was feeling could leave her indifferent.

Haven't you had enough of all this, Pascal?

I have, he said. Yes, I have had enough. But what do you want me to do? I can't let those bastards fuck up twenty years of struggle.

Antonia could not help but think that at that moment, on

the other side, someone who had shadows under his eyes just as dark as Pascal's must be thinking the exact same thing. It was absurd. But she didn't say anything.

And you, how are you? he asked.

Fine, she said, lying.

In the prayer that Christ himself taught the apostles, it is said: *Forgive us our trespasses, as we forgive those who trespass against us.* The original sentence in Greek, which the Latin liturgy preserves, should, however, have been translated as follows: *Remit us our debts as we remit them to our debtors.* This flagrant distortion may be explained by how offensive the image of a God busy with sordid accounting operations would seem. Deep down it doesn't matter. Because the people who recite this prayer regard trespasses the way they regard debts: they do not remit the latter any more than they forgive the former. While Antonia was talking with Pascal, the two sides of the nationalist movement were scrupulously recording in their ledgers every trespass, every failing, every threat, every insulting word, and everybody expected at some point to be paid back, with accrued interest, in the currency of blood.

In October 1990, the FLNC informed the press through its usual communication channels that it would be giving a press conference. It was being held near the village of Tavera. In the van taking her there with the other journalists, no one spoke to Antonia. Once they got there, she was surprised by how many militants were present. Every member of the clandestine organization seemed to be there. The jeans, military fatigues, and woolen balaclavas which had lent earlier press conferences an air of rural romanticism had disappeared. They had been replaced by black zippered jumpsuits and motorcycle hoods that seemed to conceal smooth reptilian faces with big florescent eyes. Antonia stood next to the television team's projector. She was waiting for one of the organization's spokesmen sitting at a table in the front row to begin reading the press release. At one end of the third row, almost directly opposite her, a militant gave an odd little wave of his hand, as if to say hello. She looked at him closely, and he waved again. At first she thought it must be Simon T., but it wasn't his build. She took pictures while the spokesman was reading, in a deep fine voice he did not bother to disguise. When it was over, she looked again at the militant and studied him closely. He was carrying a hunting rifle and a handgun without a holster stuffed in his belt outside his jumpsuit. Antonia recognized the model. It was a Luger parabellum P08, identical to the one her great-grandfather had brought back from Germany in 1919 when he was released from captivity, an antique they kept in a cupboard under a pile of sheets along with the bags of moth balls. It wasn't inconceivable that one of the militants might also own an old gun like that, but it was highly unlikely, particularly as the militant in question kept on sending her pathetic little greeting signs. She had to concede therefore that the man there a few yards away from her, squeezed tight into his ninja jumpsuit, could be none other than her own brother, Marc-Aurèle.

Oh, the bastard! she thought, and Marc-Aurèle was not the target of her wrath.

The next day at dawn, she jumped into her car and left for the village to look for Pascal B. She found him still in bed, which was not surprising: Tavera was a two-hour drive from there, and he must have gone to bed late.

You recruited my brother! Antonia screamed. You have no right to do that!

Pascal B. was still too sleepy to efficiently ward off Antonia's fury. He did not try to deny her accusation but in his defense said that he had merely given in to Marc-Aurèle's repeated requests. His arguments did not have the effect he'd hoped for. Well then, you shouldn't have given in! Did he give in to all the young men who, like Marc-Aurèle, let themselves be taken in by all that ridiculous mythology without having the slightest idea what it really implied? She challenged him: let him give her an example of one quality, one single quality Marc-Aurèle had that would have made his recruitment indispensable! Did he have the training of a commando member? Was he an astute political strategist? A bomb expert? A killer? What then? she shouted. What?

Don't get so worried! Pascal tried to calm her down as he got dressed. Marc-Aurèle is in no danger.

In no danger? But you told me yourself that the situation was getting dangerous! You told me yourself that it would end badly. What if they put him in jail? You're not Marc-Aurèle. He's a nice guy. He's weak. He would never be able to deal with prison—and, imagining her brother sitting on a hard mat while that huge echo of locks closing and keys jangling resounded down the corridors, she began to cry.

Pascal B. gave a sigh, hesitated for a moment, and then, after forcing her to sit down, he said: listen, he really is in no danger. I'll explain why. But you have to promise not to tell anyone.

Because I go around telling other people what you tell me? I know things, too many, as a matter of fact, things I'm not supposed to know, things I'd rather not know, but I never tell anyone.

He explained that the true purpose of the press conference had been to bring about a de facto exclusion from the movement of the entire group of their enemies: the sectors of the FLNC that they controlled had not been informed. Moreover, they did not have access to the usual communication channels. They would find out about the press conference in the newspaper that morning. So, naturally, in their absence, they'd had to swell their own ranks a little and recruit a good number of people. To make up the numbers. Marc-Aurèle had a walk-on part, he'd enjoyed it and it helped the movement, but he would never do anything else, Pascal B. gave her his word, her brother would never take part in any attacks, would never levy the revolutionary tax, they would take him out to a little meeting in the maquis from time to time, and that would be it. Antonia really needn't worry.

Does my brother know that? Does he know why you agreed to let him come?

No, of course not, Pascal B. conceded, looking away.

That is really disgusting. You have nothing to be proud of.

You're never satisfied, are you? Pascal B. remarked limply.

Antonia didn't answer. She stopped off at her parents'. Marc-Aurèle was having breakfast. She gave him a hug. You look after yourself. He was eighteen years old and as happy as a clam. So you saw me? Antonia squeezed him harder. Yes, I saw you. You take very good care of yourself.

In the weeks that followed, the militants who had been ousted held their own press conference in Tralonca. This time the press was summoned through the Canal Historique. Apparently this branch of the FLNC, which also presented itself as the only legitimate one, counted an even greater number of militants than the rival branch. Antonia realized that another unofficial recruitment campaign had just been held so that, by virtue of the miracle of even more supernatural mathematics than those governing infinite sets, their numbers had more than doubled by being divided in half.

Day by day, the situation worsened.

At the end of November, the partisans of the Canal Habituel arrived in Bastia en masse, armed to the teeth. To transfer it to Ajaccio, they loaded up all the equipment coveted by the Canal Historique for publishing the nationalist newspaper: computers, imagesetters, even office furniture. For an hour in the very center of town, the two groups confronted each other in the dark of night, their guns in their hands.

At one o'clock in the morning, Antonia's telephone rang. It was Simon T. At first Antonia thought something terrible must have happened. He never called her. Usually he waited for her to call.

Simon, are you all right? Tell me everything's okay!

He was fine. He apologized. He had just come from Bastia. He wanted to talk to someone, no, he wanted to talk to her, just to her. Could he stop by and see her? She answered that she would wait for him. He arrived ten minutes later. He looked terrible. He put his Colt 45 on the table after removing the charger and taking out the bullet that was in the barrel. He told her what had just happened in Bastia. It seemed to him that after months of an imperceptible but continuous descent into an abyss, he had just touched bottom. When they arrived, from all over Corsica, they found their allies from Bastia who had called for help barricaded inside the newspaper offices. They were being besieged by the militants of the other faction. But we had more people on our side, said Simon, way more. It was surreal. He was on a street corner together with Jean-Joseph C., his gun in his hand, a bullet in the barrel, and an old woman came by and thought they were policemen. How could she have thought the police hadn't intervened? Jean-Joseph reassured her, he was indeed a police inspector, he insisted, a chief inspector, even. We have the situation under control, Madame. We will get the better of all these hooligans, you can put your mind at rest. And the old woman went on home, not without first gratifying the brave young man with a grateful smile and a maternal little pat on the cheek. We began loading the equipment, Simon continued. The others were on the sidewalk. They didn't move. Someone told them that if one of them took so much as a single step he'd get a bullet in the head. We called them every name in the book. What could they do? At first, I was enjoying it. It always feels good to be strong. But now it makes me want to puke. Antonia thought that once again she had missed a rare opportunity to take fantastic pictures. She'd been doing a story about the departmental council instead. This really was turning into a curse.

You should have called me beforehand, I would have come with you, she said.

Simon didn't react to her remark. For months he had been trying to keep everything from collapsing, when he ran into guys from the other side he knew well, he acted as if there were nothing amiss, he wanted to believe that their political differences wouldn't change anything on a personal level, which was plain stupid because there was nothing political about the differences in question, so he would hold out his hand and stand there like an idiot with his hand in the void while they stared at him full of hatred and he too felt that hatred in return, he felt like ramming his pistol into the mouths of those men he had thought were his brothers and who now refused to shake his hand, and to smash their teeth along the way because everything he had taken for the glue of an indestructible brotherhood for years was nothing but sand, mist, not even mist, just nothing, nothing at all, and that evening, in Bastia, they had thrown every name in the book at them, had humiliated them, they couldn't help themselves, and at the time it was exhilarating, even though it was a mistake, because the stain of humiliation can never be erased, and in the great accounting ledger they had all just contracted a terrible debt they would have to pay back sooner or later. Above all, concluded Simon, above all I cannot help but wonder what they're worth, the few friendships I have left. Maybe nothing, either. Just shit.

Get up, Antonia ordered.

She pushed him toward the bed, he flopped back onto it, and she climbed astride him, pulling off the long white T-shirt she wore to sleep in.

I didn't come here for that, Simon said sadly, brushing the back of his hand against her bare breasts.

I know, Antonia answered, and she leaned over him to kiss him.

Time went by, and the tragedy Simon had been dreading

did not happen. No one went beyond the stage of invectives, rival press conferences, and the monotonous competition of attacks. At the time, to her great shame, Antonia felt almost disappointed.

In January 1991, a shower of missiles falls upon Iraq, lighting television screens with a greenish glow. Movie cameras are installed in the cockpits of American fighter jets, filming a complicated network of levers and indicators that look straight out of a flight simulator or a video game. Microphones record the pilots' swear words and cries of frenetic joy whenever their target explodes in the silence of a brief, dazzling glitter. Death has been dimmed, abolished in the innocuous space of a virtual world. Nothing is shown of what should be seen. The Americans will not repeat the mistakes they made in Vietnam twenty years earlier. No general will see his own life come to an end as surely as that of the man he is shooting in the head, because just as he is pressing the trigger, Eddie A. is releasing the shutter on his camera. No photograph will show the face of a soldier who has just looked the Gorgon straight in the eye during the Tet offensive and who stays seated, his hands on his assault rifle, so perfectly immobile that in the five successive shots taken by Donald McC. it is impossible to discern the slightest change in his expression, the slightest movement of his eyelids, as if he had been transformed into a statue.

Staring at her television, because the past is always more legible than the present, Antonia was sorry she had been born too late and in the wrong place. Everything that was familiar to her seemed, by virtue of its very familiarity, derisory, of no interest. She was incapable of casting a wise gaze on what surrounded her just then, and Simon T.'s despair, the depth and sincerity of which she did not underestimate, did not seem to her any more deserving of attention than the existential angst of an oversensitive adolescent. In the month of August, she read a very short article in the international pages about the siege that had just begun of a city whose name she didn't even know in a country she had never thought about and that would soon no longer exist. The city was called Vukovar. The fact that it was in Europe seemed insufficient to arouse the curiosity of the media, let alone the general public. Here was the opportunity Antonia had been waiting for, to do the real work of a photographer at last. In Yugoslavia, war had not yet put on its digital finery. She suggested to her superiors that she could go there and bring back an entire feature for the newspaper. Naturally, they laughed in her face. She could hardly have ignored the fact that she was working for a regional daily whose vocation was in no way to send photographers all over the world at great expense to cover incomprehensible conflicts that the local readership couldn't care less about. Antonia would do better to focus her attention on the major summer supplement, "Festival Time in Our Villages," due to come out the following week. After a brief spell of depression, she realized she didn't need the newspaper's permission to set out. She would ask for unpaid leave. She'd cover her own expenses. If need be, she'd ask her godfather for money. She had to start somewhere. Many of the photographers she admired were bound to have headed out before her without any comfortable guarantee that they would be able to sell their pictures. She was absolutely free, and the fact that this had only become clear to her now was a sign of how much her will and her intellect had been numbed by mediocrity, resignation, and routine.

At the dinner table, when she informed her family of her decision, it triggered an outburst of maternal tears and screams. How could anyone dream of going off to get killed by a horde of bloodthirsty savages when they had everything they needed at home? How could a daughter behave in such an ungrateful manner toward her parents when she had only ever received their love and protection, yet here she was condemning them to a slow death from worry? Marc-Aurèle tried to show his support—I think it's great, what you want to do, Antonia, very brave—but he was ruthlessly reduced to silence when they threatened to disown him—totally, irreversibly, and with immediate effect—which would make him a pariah scorned by all. No one would listen to any of Antonia's arguments. She gave up trying to explain.

Say whatever you like, Maman, it won't change a thing. I'm going. I came here to inform you, not to discuss it with you.

Antonia's mother went off to her bedroom. So she had no more daughter and maybe no more children at all, she added, addressing Marc-Aurèle, who prudently remained silent.

Don't worry too much, her father said. She has a tendency to overdramatize, as you well know.

I know, Papa, Antonia replied, without pointing out that the use of the verb "overdramatize" was, in this case, an enormous euphemism.

But maybe you could give it a little more thought? he asked, hopefully.

Antonia slowly shook her head.

I have thought. I've been rotting in this hole for years. I've had plenty of time to think.

He didn't try again.

I'm going to your mother, to try to calm her down a little.

Antonia went on sitting at the table with Marc-Aurèle and her godfather, who still had not said a thing.

What about you? she asked him now. What do you think?

In his entire life, he had never had the strength to tell her she was wrong, and he did not depart from the rule now. He respected her decision. He supposed it meant a lot to her. Perhaps, in her way, she, too, felt she had a calling. There are callings one must respond to. He'd be afraid for her sake, obviously, very afraid. But he would pray. With all his heart. Antonia joked about whether prayers that God clearly only paid attention to in a distracted or random fashion could do much good. He tried to laugh along with her.

I'll pray all the same.

He prayed, every day, and Antonia had come home without a scratch. Perhaps he'd asked God too often to bring her home to him alive and not often enough to make sure He also preserved her soul. Had he overlooked the most important thing? Had he thought enough about Antonia when every night he would say the closing words of the prayer taught to us by the Lord himself—*deliver us from evil*? He can no longer remember, but even if he had, this time God had not seen fit to answer his prayer.

AGNUS DEI

10
(JNA Soldiers Slaughtering Pigs, Eastern Slavonia, 1992)

Early in the month of November 1991, it was Antonia V.'s turn to arrive in Belgrade, where she has reserved a room at the Hotel Moskva. Waiters in striped vests, holding aloft trays heavy with drinks and strange pastries, scurry through the huge bar with its sofas upholstered in a cream and fir-green fabric. On this first day, Antonia V. feels so brutally disoriented by the foreignness of it all that she cannot tell whether it is enchanting or terrifying.

She has come to take pictures of the war, to keep a trace of what is happening here.

She has also come to live another life besides her own.

But for the moment, in the bar of the Hotel Moskva, the only thing that matters is the strangeness of this new life. Antonia V. cannot bring herself to think seriously about the war being fought less than ninety miles away, its hypothetical reality confirmed here only by the unusual presence of foreign reporters.

How does one get to a war? What path does one take? Is there a vestibule, a border, a door to go through, behind which the official territory of war begins?

She goes out of the hotel, taking her camera. She follows the signs pointing in the direction of Kalemegdan, she walks around the park where the cold is so biting that it makes the place feel almost exotic, she walks past the monument to France, and from the walls of the fortress she takes pictures of the confluence of the Danube and the Sava. She goes back the way she has come. The streets echo with the sounds of a Slavic language she is hearing for the first time. In the church of St. Mark, a man is standing before the icons. With every candle he lights, he makes the sign of the cross and kneels, one hand on the floor, as if he has just planted the foot of the cross there, after tracing it in the air with his fingertips.

She goes back to her room.

She writes to her godfather: *First I saw icons and an emperor's tomb.*

She goes back down to the bar and sits at a table alone. She looks so lost and inexperienced that this undoubtedly arouses the compassion of a lively group of journalists, who motion to her to join them. Which she does with an eagerness that seems utterly lacking in dignity. They are speaking English. She discovers to her horror that she hardly understands a thing.

How could she have dreamt of coming here without even first making sure she'd be able to understand what people were saying to her and to make herself understood in return?

They give her a shot of *šljivovica*. The alcohol burns her throat and her chest. A photographer in his forties sitting opposite her gets up and walks around the table to come and sit by her. He's French. This must be the first time in her life she feels like kissing someone simply because they're French. He tells her terrible, fascinating stories he has brought back from Beirut, Phnom Penh, Tehran. By the fourth or fifth glass, Antonia V. has discovered the miraculous linguistic virtues of *šljivovica*: her memories of English class at the lycée, which she had feared were gone forever, have finally surfaced, and she can make out increasingly intelligible sentences from the opaque buzz of voices around her. The Frenchman tells her he'll be going to Vukovar the following morning. She asks if she can come along.

He says: I'm not here to babysit.

Antonia V. doesn't dare say another word to him.

But how does one get to the war?

Later that evening, she meets an Italian journalist, a woman, to whom she can speak in Corsican. After a few hours' sleep, they meet again and leave Belgrade together with the sunrise. Antonia V. hears faraway explosions to begin with and sees the first JNA artillerymen. They pass Vukovar and head toward the front line, near Osijek. The sky is a transparent blue. Groups of soldiers are drinking *rakija* and smoking. Three hundred yards farther along, Antonia V. spots the dark shapes of two bodies lying in the grass. A soldier comes up to her. He speaks to her in English, two words she has no trouble understanding, *Croatians, deserters*, which he illustrates with an eloquent mime of helplessness. Antonia V. goes closer to the bodies. The first one fell face down. The second one is lying on his side, his arm held out in front of him, his palm open to the sky. On their back and chest, respectively, their fatigues are soaked with blood. She can see they have also been shot in the hands and feet.

Like Christ's wounds, she writes to her godfather.

She stretches out in the grass. She takes a close-up of that palm open to the sky, its stiff fingers, the gaping wound, earth in the fingernails.

There is nothing easier than getting to war.

That was something Dragan Đ., whom she will meet two weeks later in Vukovar, learned long before she did, one evening in May 1991, by showing up at the barracks where he is meant to start his military service. He left Vojvodina together with his older brother, who insisted on driving him to Croatia. The night before, they had been with friends, drinking to his departure, vast quantities, and both of them are suffering from a stubborn hangover which they try to banish by smoking joints and listening to music full blast. In the first Croatian villages they go through, they see groups of men armed with rifles, who stare at them and watch as they drive past. They conclude that Croats have a real passion for hunting. They see the checkerboard insignia, which instantly makes them think of the Ustaše.

They wander through town looking for the barracks, which the hashish has made impossible to find. They are unaware of how people are staring at them, their heavy gazes. They go around a corner, and, finally, there are the barracks, the gates closed. Dragan Đ.'s brother blows his horn. The gates open slightly, and a soldier sticks his head out through the opening. He looks at the car's license plate. He starts shouting at them. Are they completely crazy, driving around like that in a car registered in Vojvodina? Do they want to get a bullet in the head? Hurry up and get in here. We'll open the gates.

Dragan Đ.'s brother tells the soldier he did his military service four years earlier and he'd rather die than go into the barracks with a bunch of bastard soldiers.

Fuck off then, asshole! the soldier shouts.

Dragan Đ. takes his things and kisses his brother, who drives off, solemnly giving the soldier the finger through the open window of the car.

Dragan Đ. spends a month cooped up in the barracks. He has gotten to the war but doesn't know that yet.

On May 19, the independence of Croatia is massively approved by a referendum that is boycotted by the country's Serbian population.

One by one, the Croatian officers and conscripts decamp, to respond to the call of voices from the exterior demanding their presence. The Macedonians are next, not wanting to get caught in the middle of a confrontation that has less and less to do with them. The Slovenes left long ago. By the looks of it, preserving the unity of Yugoslavia is no longer on anyone's agenda. Through the eighteen months of his military service, Dragan Đ. will never be sure he has clearly understood what the official or hidden aims of the war actually consist of.

But it is clear that things are going badly, very badly indeed, the pace is accelerating, and it's all mixed up, 1912, 1934, 1943, the past that has remained stuck in people's throats for so long contaminating the present—the Ustaše from Jasenovac, knives and saws, partisans, and Chetniks with long hair and beards.

By the beginning of June, the situation has become untenable. What is left of the regiment abandons the barracks and withdraws to the east.

On June 25, Croatia declares its independence.

In July, Dragan Đ.'s company occupies a village in Slavonia. The Croat forces are close by, within shouting range. Neither side takes any particular precautions. The rules of engagement are not very clear, and no one is shooting. Soldiers move forward between the lines to talk to the other side. It all seems unreal. And a few weeks later, as he kneels by one of his comrades who has been shot in the lung and is gasping and drooling a suffocating pink foam, Dragan Đ. cannot understand how everything could have gone so wrong. A chain reaction of tiny, fatal steps has caused him to progress effortlessly along a path of madness that has led from a party one evening in Vojvodina to this place. He now knows that when he kissed his brother at the entrance to the barracks, he had already gotten to the war, and that there is nothing easier.

In August, then again in October, he finds himself fighting hand-to-hand.

At the beginning of November, he is promoted to sergeant. He drinks. He takes every drug he can get his hands on. It's not such a bad solution.

On the 21st, three days after the fall of Vukovar, he sees two girls walking toward his unit, one of them with a camera over her shoulder. It's been ten days now since Antonia V., who no longer needs a babysitter, began making her way back and forth along the front, together with Jelica, whose last name she doesn't know. She met her at the bar of the Hotel Moskva, where the French-speaking student was offering her services as an interpreter to the journalists. A daily and no doubt excessive consumption of *rakija* has certainly helped Antonia V. to get along in English, but her level doesn't allow for either precision or subtlety, which is also the case for the majority of Serbian and Croatian soldiers she has had to deal with up to now. Jelica's assistance has been precious. And above all, Antonia V. likes being with her.

A few days earlier, as they were driving west across a flat landscape that looked innocuous enough, they heard three shots and the frightening ping of something metallic on the left rear fender of the car. Jelica was driving. She stepped on the gas. Some assholes are shooting at us! Antonia V. couldn't believe she had just been under fire. Her heart took off, racing with terror and joy.

Why are they shooting at us? she asked Jelica. Who is it?

I don't know! It could be anybody. Whoever is shooting, maybe he doesn't even know why. We're out in the open. He has a gun. That's all. He can't help himself. Can't you see what idiots they've all become!

Jelica hunched over the steering wheel, her eyes glued to the road. She slowed down.

The assholes! she said, did you see those assholes? And suddenly she couldn't stop laughing, she had tears in her eyes, and Antonia V., laughing too, had time to lean against the passenger door and take her picture.

She loves being here with Jelica, she loves laughing when they are shot at for no reason, this feeling of falling, the dizziness, the joy of righting oneself at the last minute.

Now they are walking straight past Dragan Đ., and sudden shouts make them turn their heads. A dozen or so yards away, a man wearing a strange uniform and a black beret is admonishing a JNA officer who has his eyes lowered in the other man's presence like a naughty pupil caught out by his teacher.

Every time the officer tries to answer, the man in the beret slaps him. All the soldiers are watching the scene now, their gleeful interest obvious. Antonia V. thinks she ought to take a picture, even by guesswork, holding her camera against her hip, but she can't bring herself to, she's afraid she might be spotted, and she curses her lack of courage.

That evening in her room at the Hotel Moskva, she writes to her godfather: *I have a good eye. But my hand doesn't always follow. So then my eye serves no purpose. I've no talent.*

Who is that guy? she asks Jelica.

Who is that? Jelica asks Dragan Đ.

He replies in impeccable English: he's the leader of a group of paramilitaries. His real name is Željko R., but everyone calls him Arkan. Dragan Đ. has already crossed paths with him several times behind the lines. He'd never heard of him. He's been told that before the war this Arkan managed a club of football supporters in Belgrade. Ultras. It makes no sense. But now Arkan, in uniform, is slapping their commanding officer, and no one sees a problem with that because, after all, none of this makes any sense and the commanding officer is a heartless bastard. They would all like to slap him.

Before long, Antonia V. will come upon a first photograph taken by Ron H., in Erdut, where Arkan is posing with a baby tiger in his hand, in front of his men assembled on a tank and, a year later, a second photograph taken in Bosnia with that sort of insane courage she does not have—she can no longer deny it—and probably never will have.

They enter Vukovar. Dragan Đ. goes with them. You cannot even say it is a city in ruins. It is an unbelievable pile of rubble, twisted metal, and dust, where JNA soldiers roam alongside a few gaunt civilians risen from an underground hell.

It's like in a film, Jelica says.

A large solitary section of wall already covered in Cyrillic writing stands amid the ruins in incongruous solitude. Dragan points to some of the graffiti and starts laughing. He translates: *Please, guys, be kind, leave me standing!* Next to it is written in enormous capital letters: *Only death.* No way of knowing whether this is a desperate observation or a nihilistic slogan. Antonia V. takes a picture of the wall. Once again she fears her photograph will be a falsehood, imparting a depth steeped in meaning that doesn't actually exist.

All three return to Dragan Đ.'s unit, and he offers them a glass of the inevitable *rakija*. A bit farther along, Croatian prisoners are climbing into the back of a truck covered with a tarpaulin. Antonia V. takes a few photos. No one pays her the slightest attention. Just once, a prisoner turns to face her lens with a terrified gaze that makes her shudder. She presses the shutter release.

Ever since she arrived, both sides of the front line, with the same tremor in their voices, have been telling her invariably bleak stories about refined acts of violence and murder to illustrate the enemy's sadism. Oddly, these stories of pleading children killed by ruthless executioners, or of pregnant women, their bellies gleefully ripped open, are sometimes virtually identical, give or take a detail or two. All these stories are false, of course, each in its own way. Some of them have been traveling through time since 1912, 1934, or 1943, transformed and enriched along the way to acquire an abominable precision. Others are completely made up, like the legends of ogres and monsters that feed childhood nightmares.

But the horrible things that really happen, no one tells those stories, she writes to her godfather.

In the week that follows, she accompanies Dragan Đ.'s unit to the Slavonian front. She has decided against going to either the Croatian side, or to the Serbs in Krajina. Up to now she has not managed to sell even a single photograph. She thinks she might have more luck if she sticks to the coherence of a single point of view.

She takes a picture of Dragan Đ. lying in the grass, his eyes haunted, his Kalashnikov lying across his chest. In Serbia, the reservists and conscripts hide to avoid conscription. No relief troops have come. All available soldiers are put to use, to exhaustion.

I was called up too soon, says Dragan Đ. I didn't understand what was going on. If I'd known what sort of shit I was in for, I would've gone to Hungary. I have cousins on my mother's side in a village not far from Szeged. It's a dump, but it has to be better than here.

In December, Antonia V. goes back to Corsica for the holidays. She takes the opportunity to ask her bank for a loan: she'll reimburse it when she's sold her photographs. She hardly answers her parents' questions. Despite her best efforts, she cannot bridge the invisible gap that seems to separate her from her loved ones.

In January, even though a cease-fire—constantly violated— has been announced, she is back at the bar in the Hotel Moskva, and her joy at being there is totally disproportionate. Jelica is now working for other journalists. They meet up every evening. They go for drinks, eat out at restaurants.

Antonia catches up with Dragan Đ.'s unit in a village on the banks of the Drava. He's not there. She's afraid he might be wounded, or dead. They assure her he isn't. While he is indeed at the military hospital, it is only because he became depressed, due no doubt to physical and nervous exhaustion.

Not really, he explains upon his return. I was taking too many drugs, that's all. They didn't demote me. They just told me to stop messing around.

She's glad to see him again.

On January 20, 1992, he takes the lead in a reconnaissance patrol. Antonia V. goes with him. She takes pictures of the column advancing across the flat white land. The snow obliterates perspective, and Antonia V. is afraid that her shots, too wide, won't come out. In the afternoon, they enter a hamlet with four or five houses. At first, they see nothing more than a few compact forms busy around a mass of colored spots. The soldier at the front of the column comes to a halt, then suddenly bends over and throws up. A dozen corpses are lying in the snow, mostly women. Pigs are moving avidly from one corpse to the next, grunting. They got out of their pen—unless whoever did this went to the trouble of letting them out, knowing exactly what would happen.

Antonia V. has a vague memory of a cruel fairy tale she might have heard long ago, or a nightmare, full of light and garish colors, before the relief of awakening in darkness.

She goes closer, looking through the viewfinder. Now she feels astonishingly calm and lucid. She takes pictures of the corpses, the pigs, the trails of blood in the snow.

She hears Dragan Đ. shouting something wildly.

Four or five soldiers stand in a line and begin firing, shouting insults, prayers, swear words. Antonia V. kneels down in the snow. She sets up her shot, the barrels of their assault rifles are aimed slightly toward the ground, she hears the squealing of the wounded pigs as they fall heavily into the snow, she sees the fabric of a skirt.

She takes more pictures.

A soldier is running, firing at a huge boar that is trying to get away until it, too, falls. The soldier goes closer and empties his charger. Dragan Đ. is standing in the snow, his features contorted, a pistol in his hand.

When they get back, everyone immediately reaches for the *rakija* bottles. Antonia V. still feels very calm. She empties her glass.

Have you seen *Apocalypse Now*? Dragan Đ. asks her.

She nods.

Me, too. The Doors and all the rest . . .

He shakes his head and refills his glass.

We know it's not like that at all, he concludes. Not at all.

At four o'clock in the morning, she awakes with a start in the soothing darkness of her room at the Hotel Moskva. Her camera is at the foot of the bed. She thinks about what her rolls of film contain, and cannot get back to sleep.

She writes to her godfather: *It's not true that it's like a film.*

She goes down for breakfast. She sits next to a correspondent from a French newspaper she's met several times already. She tells him what happened the day before. She tells him about the pictures she took. The shock they will certainly produce, if they're published. He tries gently to set her right. No photographs, no articles to date have produced any shock other than, perhaps, the useless and ephemeral shock of horror or compassion. People don't want to see this, and if they do see it, they would rather forget. It's not that they're mean, or selfish, or indifferent. At least not only that. But it's impossible to look at things like this knowing there's strictly nothing you can do. We don't have the right to expect that of them. The only thing that is in their power is to look away. They feel indignant. And then they look away.

So what is the point of us being here?

Someone has to do it.

But above all, she writes to her godfather, *they like it, they really like it, all of them, and so do I.*

For two days, she doesn't go back to the front. She wanders around the streets of Belgrade, where war seems like an insubstantial dream. In the evening, she goes out with Jelica.

She is beginning to think she has seen something it would have been infinitely preferable for her not to have seen because now she can no longer look away. And yet it is only a tiny event, a stammer, the insignificant episode of a story that did not begin here and will not end here because it has neither beginning nor end. She tells none of this to her godfather.

She simply writes: *I know that certain things must remain hidden.*

Be that as it may, several of the pictures she has taken are doomed to remain hidden because they are indeed unbearable, and it would be easy to believe they are straight out of a horror film—even if *it's not like that at all, not at all.* Others are less explicit but every bit as obscene. They show nothing, but what they suggest is dead obvious, and, in a way, that is even worse. All these precautions, the subtleties of framing, the clear conscience of what is left off-camera, the repulsive sense of propriety, the pleasure.

There are so many ways to appear obscene, she writes to her godfather.

She will not develop her rolls of film.

She goes one last time to the front. She tells Dragan Ð. that she is going home. She has taken enough pictures of the war. She'll come back in November, when he finishes his military service. If he agrees, she'll go with him on his journey home.

In November? he asks.

Yes. So he has to look after himself in the meantime, because she will need him to be there. If he's not there in November when she comes back, the feature she would like to shoot will be completely ruined.

In Belgrade, she goes out one last evening with Jelica. They get back at dawn, completely drunk. Outside the Hotel Moskva, they hug each other for a long time in the icy cold to say goodbye.

Antonia V. resumes her work at the local paper that hired her back in 1984. She takes innocuous, insignificant photographs where it does not matter whether they are hidden or shown. She puts money aside. No one criticizes her for her useless trips, and no one asks why none of her photographs have appeared in the press. She talks to her godfather, in the vaguest of terms, about what she witnessed in Yugoslavia. She sticks to edifying commonplaces about the horrors of war. Perhaps he has guessed what she was not able to tell him.

Ron H.'s second photo is published. On it, one can see one of Arkan's men getting ready to kick three Bosnian civilians he has just gunned down. The paramilitary looks very young. He is wearing sunglasses with a white frame pushed up on his head, clearly indicating that the picture does not belong to history but to current news. He is leaning on his left leg, his body tilted slightly backward, his right leg bent, ready to kick. In his left hand he is holding a cigarette between loosely spread fingers, his gesture one of elegant, aristocratic negligence. A man and two women are lying on the sidewalk, fresh blood glistening. It is impossible to tell which of the bodies the paramilitary is about to kick.

Antonia V. shows her godfather the picture.

It's a sin, he murmurs.

It's a waste of time, Antonia says. Nobody gives a damn.

And that, too, is a sin, her godfather adds. The sin of the world.

In April, the siege of Sarajevo begins, and for four years it will be broadcast live, a steady accompaniment to people's evening meals.

In early November, Antonia V. goes back to the Hotel Moskva, now empty of journalists. Things are getting bad, coming to a head, on every side at once, everything is too hard to follow, and they've all gone to Bosnia. When she finds Dragan Đ., he has lost a lot of weight. He gives her a weak smile. She wonders what he has seen. She wonders what he has done.

The day of his demobilization, she follows him as he goes around carrying out the administrative procedures that set him free and restore him to his past life, a life he will, however, never find again. The plan is for him to be taken back to Belgrade on a military bus. From there, he'll go home using regular public transport. He asks the driver if he'll agree to let Antonia V. come along. The driver grumbles something.

He doesn't give a damn, Dragan Đ. translates.

But she understood.

The bus is almost empty. In addition to Antonia V. and Dragan Đ. there are only four passengers: three soldiers and a paramilitary who is carrying a pair of suitcases so full they're about to burst. The bus drives through the low-lying country-side. At one checkpoint, they are stopped by the military police, who ask them to get out and open their luggage.

The paramilitary takes one of the policemen by the arm and pulls him to one side. He speaks to him for a moment, patting him on the shoulder. The policeman nods vigorously. The paramilitary takes something out of one of his suitcases and gives it to the policeman, who shakes his hand and motions to him to get back on the bus.

Now the policemen turn to Dragan Đ. They search his duffel bag, taking out the cassettes and two books they wave in his face before tossing them to the ground. They are laughing. Antonia V. knows she ought to be taking pictures, but once again she doesn't dare. She thinks about Ron H. She holds up her camera as discreetly as possible. She takes the pictures.

She gets back on the bus and sits next to Dragan Đ. He is trembling as if he had a fever. He takes her wrist. They're bastards, he says, assholes from Belgrade. Look at me, look at the state I'm in, look at these disgusting fatigues I'm wearing. I've been at the front, for fuck's sake. They ought to be giving me a medal. But those guys don't give a damn, with their fucking shiny clean uniforms, they treat me like a piece of shit. Because I have nothing to give them, and they don't like it. Did you see what they did with my books? That's who's running the country now. Football supporters and morons who throw books on the ground. Why are you reading this stupid Hungarian? they asked me. Why are you reading this stupid Pole? To those guys, Bukowski is a stupid Pole. Bastards. Bastards.

By the time they reach Belgrade, he has stopped talking. They take another bus. They follow the course of the Danube.

They walk through the streets of a town she does not know. Dragan Đ. stops on a bridge. Some adolescent boys make fun of him. Antonia V. takes one more picture, and then it's over. He leaves, by himself, wiping away his tears. He doesn't want her to go with him. He doesn't want to share with her what will happen from that moment on, and she lets him go, even though she would like so much to be able to say goodbye.

She goes back to the bus station and to Belgrade. She calls Jelica to ask her to spend the evening with her. She waits for her at the bar of the Hotel Moskva, on the sofas upholstered in cream and fir-green fabric, drinking a *šljivovica*. She thinks about those boys, how they laughed on the bridge. She understands nothing.

That, too, is a sin, her godfather would have said.

She doesn't believe in sin. She doesn't even know what it is. But while drinking her *šljivovica*, she feels increasingly uncomfortable with the idea of publishing the photographs she took today. Even if the magazine did accept them, which is highly unlikely, she doesn't want a stranger's eyes to look with curiosity or indifference on the complete disaster she witnessed today. She does not want to duplicate that disaster.

There are so many ways to appear obscene, she once wrote to her godfather.

Tomorrow she'll go home, she'll leave forever this land with all its temporary names, and today's rolls of film will join all the others waiting in a cardboard box, film she will never develop.

She doesn't believe in sin, nor does she believe in the Lamb of God who taketh away the sin of the world. But at least, as long as it is in her power, she, Antonia V., will add nothing to what that world already is.

COMMUNION: *LUX ÆTERNA*

11
(Young Newlyweds Running in the Sunset, Mauritius, 1997)

For years, except for when he was in prison, Antonia had slept with Pascal B. using no form of contraception other than the withdrawal method—one that had long been shown to have contributed substantially to the increase in the birthrate and that her partner practiced, moreover, with a purely relative dexterity—but in all those years, she had never gotten pregnant. Yet now that she had been taking the pill with military rigor, she found herself in a sordid hospital office opposite some harpy who was trying to persuade her not to have an abortion and looking at her with patent disgust from the moment she realized she would not succeed. Apparently, everyone on the planet thought they were entitled to share their opinion regarding Antonia's decision. It had started with her own weakness, calling Simon T. after she got back from Yugoslavia to ask him to spend the night with her, then continued with her stupidity in informing him of the burdensome consequences of their encounter; now he too behaved as if she owed him an explanation.

Is it because of Yugoslavia? Is that why?

The question had exasperated Antonia. Her refusal to have a child could only be pathological, so she must be hiding some traumatic experience that would throw light on the irrational nature of her behavior. But Antonia had never been more rational. Despite her best efforts, she could find no reason to carry the pregnancy to term. She cut the conversation short.

I'm under no obligation to discuss this with you. I'm

informing you, that's all. And I was under no obligation to do that, either.

He reacted as if she had hit him. He said something categorical and needlessly dramatic, then turned on his heels and marched out.

Antonia was admitted to the hospital one morning in January 1993. The doctor received her with a thoughtfulness she hadn't expected. The anesthesiologist leaned over her, chose a vein in which to plant her needle, and asked her to start counting. It took her some time to emerge from her artificial sleep. Whenever she opened her eyes, a powerful hand pushed her backward into a world where hazy shadows danced, and her eyelids closed again. She felt as if she were being held prisoner in an extremely unpleasant place somewhere between waking and unconsciousness. When at last she managed to emerge, her mouth was dry, and her belly hurt. Simon T. was sitting next to the bed, apparently in the depths of despair.

Why are you looking so glum? she asked, her voice barely audible.

I was here when they brought you back, he replied. You were agitated; you were trying to speak, and you were crying. It was really rough.

It's the anesthesia, she said. I had nightmares. How did you know it was today?

I asked Madeleine. He held her hand. She found the strength to smile at him, then fell asleep again. He took her home that afternoon. She didn't see him again until summer.

She did her work, went out, visited her parents, refrained from calling Simon, even when her desire to became almost painful, and from time to time she allowed herself a brief affair so that she would have something going on in her life.

She no longer dreamt of producing anything more than images as ephemeral as the paper they were printed on every morning and which, every evening, if it wasn't used to light the fire in the fireplace, ended up in a garbage can along with vegetable peels, coffee grounds, and cigarette butts. She didn't complain. She had no right to, nor did she have the strength. Or even the desire. Because there were basically only two categories of professional photographs: the ones that should never have existed in the first place, and the ones that deserved to disappear, which meant that the existence of photography itself could clearly not be justified, but since Antonia had made it her profession and didn't know how to do anything else, she would simply have to devote herself to one of the two categories. So she devoted herself to the second one, and she accepted it, not the way one assumes a choice, but rather the way one yields to the indisputable authority of a fact.

In August 1993, the Canal Historique of the FLNC delivered a press release at a public meeting in Corte, and in it they claimed responsibility for the assassination in the month of June of a turncoat militant from their own side, in the name of the concept, curious to say the least, of *preventive legitimate defense*. When the delegate at the rostrum had finished reading, the crowd gathered there beneath the marquee began to applaud. Antonia took pictures of raised hands and enthusiastic faces united in joy. She mused that it would be interesting to take a picture of someone who, in the midst of all that general jubilation, was not applauding. But other than the reporters covering the event like herself, she could see no one. She set off back to Ajaccio. She listened to music while she was driving. Only once she had reached the Vizzavona pass did she manage to shake off the psychological and intellectual paralysis she'd been living in for months. At last she realized the gravity of what was going on, and she had to pull over to the side of the road. Again she saw the damp warm flesh of hands raised in frenzied momentum, the sharp sound of clapping— and the image of other hands came to her, stiffened by the cold and by death, dirty fingers spread in a wreath around a purplish mark—then she saw again the shining eyes, the tense bodies, the ecstasy of these people transfigured by faith, happy to be there as one, to feel in unison the shared, delicious shiver that came with their total endorsement of execution, their shared adoration for the murderers, and Antonia felt unclean from having been near them, as if she'd been made to plunge into a septic tank, and she felt like throwing up. That, too, is sin, her godfather would surely say, that was all he knew how to say, and she felt like shouting in reply, yes, that, too, if you like, but the worst, the most disgusting thing of all is faith, their faith and yours, too. From that moment on, she was convinced that everything would start to go sideways and could only, once again, get worse, and go on getting worse, yet she could not tell how it would unfold, and for the first time she considered the future of her island with a terror exempt of any condescension, because from a place where people applaud their peers for claiming responsibility for murder, one can only expect the worse.

Once she got to Ajaccio, she stopped off at the newspaper offices to develop the photographs, which seemed perfectly innocent, pictures of people applauding and smiling; she alone could see how hideous they were. There was clearly no way around it: her photographs always suffered from an excess or deficit of meaning.

She called Simon T. She needed to see him.

She told him what had happened, but he already knew.

The worst, she said, was that in their place, all of you would have applauded, too, every single one of you. Then she added: no, not all. You, Simon, I think you wouldn't have applauded, I'm not sure, but I think not—and this was without a doubt the greatest compliment she had ever paid him, perhaps, even, the only one.

It is, at any rate, the only one he remembers.

Hold me, she said, stop me from thinking about all that.

Was she right? Would he not have applauded? When things really did get as ugly as they could, two years later, and the stupid war finally broke out after its long gestation period, what did he do other than accept it, without the slightest gesture of defiance? He did not protest, did nothing to try and make things right, not because things obviously could not be made right and he knew he was powerless, but simply because it didn't even occur to him. Was it fear and despair that prevented him back then from thinking, or was it the deeply rooted consent he had given during the events, in spite of his fear and despair? When Xavier S. announced that he was leaving the movement because it was out of the question for him to be part of any of it, Simon did not think that Xavier was not as stupid as he appeared after all; on the contrary, he was angry with him and was even on the verge of publicly accusing him of cowardice. However, he himself had been afraid for many long months. So often he had wanted to run away. During the terrible summer of 1995, he showed up at Antonia's place with a huge bruise on his forehead. He had gone to the bakery to buy some bread. He had just paid for the two baguettes he'd wedged under his arm and was walking toward the door when he realized that everyone was staring at him, as if on high alert, he couldn't figure out why, this was completely abnormal, he looked around and tried to identify where a threat might be coming from, apparently invisible only to him. There was an expression of stunned apprehension on the customers' faces that terrified him, he looked at them, not understanding, what are you doing? someone asked, and he felt for his gun then suddenly heard a very loud noise and everything went black, he realized he was lying on the floor, that's it, he thought, I've been shot, I'm going to die here, but he was alive after all, and when he got his wits about him, he realized that instead of walking toward the door, he had headed straight for the glass window and crashed right into it, head first, without making a single gesture to cushion the shock. He went on sitting there for a moment, completely out of it, next to the baguettes and the gun which had fallen to the floor. As a rule, misadventures of this sort elicit shared peals of laughter, but no one laughed, and when he told Antonia the story, she didn't laugh either, because she knew it wasn't funny.

Have they not all lived in abjectness?

Even if he believed in God, Simon T. would not get up to take communion. Only five individuals are walking down the central aisle of the church, around the coffin, toward the priest who is waiting for them, the chalice in his hand, five old women with Simon's mother, Damienne T., among them. She closes her eyes and lifts her face to Antonia's godfather, who places the host on her tongue. *The body of Christ.* Simon does not doubt that his mother can receive it without being guilty of blasphemy.

The choir sings: *May light eternal shine upon them, O Lord,* but it was only the light of the month of August 1993 that woke Simon when Antonia was already dressed and ready to go. She came and sat next to him and ran her hand through his hair. Do you really think I wouldn't have applauded? Yes, she answered. But I'm not sure. She kissed him. Lock the door and leave the keys in the mailbox for me. She went to work. The Canal Historique's claim of responsibility had provoked a few reactions of indignation or support, but naturally after two weeks had gone by no one remembered any of those reactions. Antonia had no illusions. She knew that they could expect nothing but the usual triumph of apathy, but she for one could not stand it. In the months that followed, she fell back into her routine. She sometimes imagined that in the end there wouldn't be any collective tragedy. Things would simply remain as foul as they already were. But she had a nagging feeling she was mistaken and that it was only a question of time.

She continued to watch and wait for photographs that ought not to exist but that she could not look away from. That same year, a South African photographer, Kevin C., won the Pulitzer Prize for one of them. On it, a child with skeletal limbs and a swollen belly is lying on the ground, and poised behind him is a vulture, staring at him with its empty eyes. In no time at all, photomontages were making the rounds, with Kevin C.'s head replacing the vulture's. Indignant right-thinking souls reproached him for having pressed the shutter rather than helping the child. To Antonia, the photograph was indisputably obscene, and so it must have seemed to Kevin C. himself, and it was no doubt for that reason that he had taken it, so that no one could claim to ignore the obscenity of the world in which they consented to live. As for Kevin C., he did not consent for very much longer. Perhaps he could no longer bear having to look the Gorgon in the eyes so often. In July 1994, at the age of thirty-three, he attached a rubber hose to his car's exhaust pipe, and run the other end through the window to where he was sitting. He left a strange letter of farewell, a confused statement about depression, debts, alimony, massacres, dying children, and torturers, and finally about a photographer friend who'd been shot dead in a township in April and whom he was hoping to see again in the eternal light.

Antonia showed her godfather the photograph: his unbearably naïve optimism appeared to her to be a particularly perverse form of consent given to the obscenity of the world.

My God! he said.

Then: What am I supposed to say?

Nothing, she replied. There is nothing you can say.

However, in 1995, when she was already weary of going from one crime scene to the next to keep a tally of the dead for the newspaper, he was the only one who reacted with something besides complicit resignation or even secret joy, because at the time it seemed to Antonia that the entire island was resounding with frenetic applause. She was covering a militant's funeral in a village in the region, the fourth or fifth victim of the now open warfare among nationalists. Her godfather had just celebrated the mass and was blessing the coffin outside the church. As soon as he had finished, four men in balaclavas appeared out of the maquis, read a text, and shot off three salvos, standing to attention, then disappeared again. Naturally Antonia had captured the scene. Her godfather came over to her. He looked outraged.

Did you know this was going to happen?

Not really, she replied. But I suspected it might, it wasn't hard to predict.

He went over to a group of militants and began telling them off in terms Antonia only partially grasped but whose vehemence left no doubt. She walked over. The militants seemed sorry the priest had not been told ahead of time, but nothing could calm her godfather down: it's a good thing you didn't tell me! Because I would never have agreed to you making such a spectacle outside the church! And the term "spectacle," which in this context could only be meant in a pejorative way, was, naturally, not to the liking of one of the militants, who objected loudly to its use and spoke of honoring a fallen comrade, but Antonia's godfather interrupted him with renewed vehemence: honor? What honor? You think there is a reason to honor him? You ought to be weeping with sadness, sadness and shame, because there's nothing to be proud of, believe me! The militant tried to answer back and made the mistake of giving a hypothetical turn to his phrase, so that it sounded like a possible threat, and this compelled Antonia's godfather to go up to him with a vague gesture that could not be qualified for certain as violent but that was judged sufficiently ambiguous by those who were watching for Antonia to shout, "Godfather!" and for two men to step between the priest and the group of militants as if they were a bunch of drunkards death would remain a mystery because, at the time, no one believed anything could happen to them, not Xavier S., nor Jean-Joseph C., nor Simon T., nor Antonia, nor any of those whom her godfather had known as children, dancing the tango, drinking Get 27 then pathetically throwing up over by the wattle fence, and who now, dazed with sorrow, were standing together by the coffin of this man he'd also known as a child, a man he'd so long feared would make his goddaughter unhappy, something which had now and for always become impossible. Antonia's godfather walked around the coffin, the censer in his hand, thinking that he did not want, ever again, to have to lay to rest someone he'd known as a child. If he stayed here, however, he would have to do it again. Because nothing changed, nothing ended, nothing began. It was like a virus, some indestructible form of malaria, whose symptoms were strong and intermittent bouts of fever, sometimes fatal, that during periods of remission simply waited to re-emerge and take new victims just when they thought they were in the clear. Pascal B. had certainly thought he was in the clear for a long time, probably since the end of 1996, when he had gathered all his friends together to announce, I've had it, it's over, refusing to give them the reasons behind his decision, a decision no one could have imagined might be due to fear, and Simon T. was sure that Pascal B. had found something out that so deeply offended his moral integrity that he could now call it quits without hesitation after an entire life of danger and sacrifice, but out of a sense of loyalty or shame he could not reveal what that deep offense was, and Simon T. had so much faith in him that he in turn said, then I've had it, too, it's over. Do what you like, Pascal B. added, addressing the others, you're free. I'm not asking you to do anything. You don't owe me anything. I'm sorry to have dragged you into this shit, and he left the meeting, with Simon T. at his heels, and he said to him again, his voice breaking with remorse, it's our fault, all of this, we're

the ones who have done this, applying to himself almost ver-
batim the words of reproach Antonia had used after three men
were shot dead in two days, on August 30 and 31, 1995. Among
them was Pierre A., lying on the sidewalk in the center of
Bastia, Antonia could still see him young and alive, standing in
the dock during the trial in Lyon, and the two images were
indissolubly associated, even though it was impossible to visu-
alize the path that led from one to the other. It was a shock to
Antonia, and she was deeply upset. She went to the village,
where she found Pascal B. devastated by sadness, but she didn't
give a damn for his sadness because it was his fault, his and all
his comrades', it was because of their stupid balaclavas and
press conferences and weapons and their entire shit mythology
that the entire island worshipped murderers now, because of
them, the capacity to deal out death had become the only
benchmark of human worth, and when Pascal B., with tears in
his eyes, told her that it had always been like that, she shouted,
that's no excuse, it's gotten even worse because of you, and this
is your crowning moment, now at last you've started killing
each other the way you've dreamt of doing for years, deep
down you must all be really happy now, at last you have the
opportunity to kill and die like men because for you that's
what it takes to be a man, you cannot even imagine it could be
anything else, much good may it do you, and if you were the
only ones concerned, I wouldn't give a fuck, but you're not
the only ones concerned, you're contaminating us, infecting
us with your rot, she shouted, everyone could hear the sound
of gunfire but it wasn't just sound waves that went through
the air, it was toxic radiation, with every shot, destroying bodies and minds, poisoning the air everyone had to breathe,
preparing God-knows-what monstrous mutation for the
future, and whenever Antonia went to a crime scene, she drew
dangerously near the radioactive source that contaminated
them all, she felt it physically, and it's all your fault, and Pascal

B. had eventually started shouting, too, you think I don't know that? You think I wouldn't like to start all over and do things differently? You think I don't know that? Don't you know me at all, then? Antonia's anger subsided all at once. It's not true that I wouldn't give a fuck, she said. I don't want them to kill you.

But in the end, they had killed him, almost before her very eyes.

In June 1999, it had been two years since she'd resigned her job and left Ajaccio to move back to the region where she was born. She'd opened a little shop with a window display of wedding photographs, and she was renting an apartment near the harbor. For two months, she'd been watching them on television, the NATO jets bombing the country which for four more years would be known as Yugoslavia. Every day, demonstrators went down into the streets of Belgrade with a paper target pinned to their chests, and the monument to France was now covered with a black sheet. Antonia would have liked to have news of Jelica, but she realized she didn't even know her last name. It would probably have been easier to find Dragan. She didn't even try. She was afraid that neither one of them would want to speak to her. What could she have said to them? All she could do was hope nothing had happened to them. That day, she was supposed to meet Pascal B. at his restaurant at five o'clock, where he was waiting for a delivery. It's been a while since we spent any time together, he'd said to her. If you want, we could go and have dinner in Bonifacio, or even in the mountains, whatever you'd like. She was heading toward the restaurant when she heard the popping sound of gunfire, familiar enough that she didn't need to wonder for long exactly what it was. She began to run, and as she was running, she already knew. She got to the restaurant less than two minutes later. The room was full of crates of food, and on the bar counter was an open account book, the pages splashed with squeezed against her eyelids, and then she yanked off her soiled clothing and went to sit in the shower. She stayed motionless in the stream of hot water, with the bar of soap in her hand. Hadn't they been safe, all of them, for a long time now, she'd believed it, oh, how stupid she'd been to believe it! They had all been there together at Xavier S. and Laetitia O.'s wedding, it was a magnificent day in February 1997, clear and cold, and it was all over, Antonia was taking pictures, Xavier S. was strutting around in a ghastly wedding suit with satin lapels, Laetitia O., five months pregnant, looked like a fat, radiant meringue, the couple had settled in a resort on the east coast where Xavier S. and his local associates ran a fashionable nightclub, gleefully rubbing shoulders with the jet set—famous singers, television presenters, politicians who had second homes in the area and whose autographed portraits were now all over Xavier's living room walls. One week after the wedding, Antonia got a call from Laetitia inviting her to come and see them. One of their famous friends had a proposal to make to her. He had adored the pictures Antonia had taken at the wedding, and while they were drinking the apéritif at Xavier S. and Laetitia O.'s house, he raved about her work. His own wedding was planned for the beginning of April, in Mauritius. If Antonia would agree to come and cover the ceremony, he was prepared to call—right away and in her presence—the photographer he'd already hired and send him packing. Of course he would take care of all Antonia's travel expenses in addition to what he paid for her work. The amount he quoted was so extravagant that Antonia thought she'd misheard. She accepted his offer. She was still reimbursing the loan she'd had to take out to finance her trips to Yugoslavia. And she wouldn't mind a change of air. Back in Ajaccio, she looked into what wedding photographers were charging. Although it was much less than what Xavier S.'s friend had offered her, Antonia worked out that, so long as she had regular work, it would provide her with a much better income than her job as a journalist. And besides, Xavier S. knew other celebrities who would surely be getting married, each wedding more splendid than the next, and who might also call on her services. The prospect of leaving one shit job for another did not exactly fill Antonia with enthusiasm, but she was prepared to jump on any way out she could find. Apathy was again expanding its reign. As if nothing had happened, the nationalists were going around putting up posters in support of political prisoners. One of them depicted a little boy, all alone and looking out to sea, and he had written "Daddy" in Corsican in the sand. His father's face appeared in a bubble above his head. The designer had given the father such a sinister expression that no rational human being could contemplate the possible liberation of such a primate without a shiver of horror, not even his son. The same old rhetoric, the same picture book. But Antonia felt irradiated. These last few years had left an indelible trace on her. She never wanted to have to go to a crime scene again. And she only knew how to do one thing in life: take pictures. She handed in her resignation.

She arrived in Mauritius, where Xavier S.'s friend welcomed her at a gorgeous hotel by the sea. He introduced her to his fiancée and to the wedding guests as an exceptionally talented photographer. He had reserved a little independent villa for her with a private pool. Never in her life had Antonia been around such luxury. She got her bearings, went for a walk on the beach, which looked just like the ones on the postcards, and drank cocktails concocted by an affable Indian barman. Only the hotel staff gave her an idea of the island's ethnic diversity, because the clientele consisted exclusively of affluent Europeans whose remarkable vulgarity was a constant source of amazement to Antonia. She photographed the wedding ceremony, the exchange of rings celebrated by the appearance of a group of undulating Creole dancers in colorful cotton skirts, and she was careful to take a portrait of every guest. The gilded sunset hour, obviously, was devoted to the young newlyweds. Antonia shot them on the beach in languid poses. A grotesque idea suddenly came to her that she was sure would delight them. She asked them to take off their shoes and run toward her along the shore, at the edge of the waves, holding hands. The groom rolled his suit trousers up on his hairy calves. They began running. Antonia asked them to do it again. They came toward her again. They were pink and sweating. Let's do it two or three more times, said Antonia. I think it will be terrific, but I want to be absolutely sure. The light changes all the time. She let her victims go half an hour later when the sun dipped below the horizon and deprived her of the pretext to invent any new form of torture. She sent the prints to the groom. He called her to reiterate how much he admired her work. His wife joined him in expressing her gratitude and recognition. Antonia went on taking wedding pictures. It was all over, nothing bad could ever happen again. Oh, how stupid she had been, she thought, sitting in the streaming water, how stupid she had been!

She got out of the shower. She scrubbed the floor and put her laundry in the washing machine. She unplugged her landline and switched off her cell phone. She went and lay down. A knocking at her door woke her up. It was seven o'clock in the morning, and she had slept a dreamless sleep as if there were nothing left inside her. She got dressed and went to open the door. Her godfather was standing there before her. My little niece, he murmured. My sweet girl. For the first time in a long time, she collapsed in his arms. During the day, she went up to the village. She stopped off to see her parents. Marc-Aurèle was in the kitchen, weeping. She went to offer her condolences to Pascal B.'s family. The date for the funeral had not yet been set. The body would be returned to them after the autopsy. All Antonia's childhood friends were there, sitting on the chairs lined up along the walls of the darkened living room. She went out, accompanied by Simon T. They walked together through the village streets. If she had not had an abortion, her child would be almost six years old and would be walking there with them, holding her hand. It was the first time such an image entered her mind. She had done the right thing, preventing this child's birth. She nearly said to Simon, Even now, don't you think I did the right thing?, but kept silent, not to hurt him. She asked something else. Should we go and have dinner in town? I can't take any more of this. He agreed. They had a drink by the harbor, then went to the restaurant. They ate on the terrace overlooking the sea.

I feel as if I were dead, said Antonia.

You're not dead, Simon said.

She shrugged and ran her hand over her face. He looked at her with boundless pity. He would have done anything to free her from her sorrow. He took her hand, and she surrendered it, completely limp, into his.

Do you want me to stay with you tonight? he asked, and he saw her eyes fill with tears while she squeezed his hand.

Yes, she said. Please, stay with me.

ABSOLVED: *LIBERA ME*

12
(*Legionnaire on a Beach near Calvi, 2003*)

D*eliver me, O Lord, from death eternal,*
and he hears it now, it is indeed Antonia's voice resounding for the last time through the church, the song rising from her broken jaw, she is a little girl again, she is confronting something that is too great, that she does not understand and that frightens her, that she can no longer escape,

Dread and trembling have laid hold on me,

she says, and she can no more find consolation than the baby crying when the too-cold water from the baptismal font spills across its brow, loving embraces, caresses, and kisses are of no use, for now nothing else exists in the world but the biting cold, fear, and solitude, and radical helplessness, don't be afraid, little one, he would like to tell her, but she cannot hear him, she is blind and deaf, she moans, he hears her moan in the solemn beauty of the singing that is also the bottomless pit, she cannot smell the incense, its wreaths curling around the coffin while her godfather slowly swings the censer and murmurs the prescribed words,

Let my cry come unto Thee, take her soul from us, O Lord,

the heavy swaying of the censer diffusing the perfume that sanctifies the flesh that God fashioned in His own image and likeness, despite the broken ribs and jaw, the inertia of frozen blood, the corruption, even if the poor thing lying at the altar already no longer resembles the young woman who, a few days earlier, was walking down the streets of Calvi to join Dragan,

whom she had feared lost and who is waiting for her, in his uniform, at the terrace of a café in the harbor, and he smiles to her
when she sits down next to him, whereas the last time she saw
him he was weeping and gesturing to her not to follow him
across that bridge over the Danube, that bridge that after the
NATO bombings, he tells her, had only motionless pillars left
standing in the current, breaking through the surface of the
dark waters, so that the great river itself seemed to be in ruins.
Adolescent boys were laughing, and she did not know why,
even though it was obvious they were laughing at Dragan, cruelly, to make fun of him, as if there were something ridiculous
or irresistibly comical about his solitary presence on the
bridge, his torn fatigues and his distress, and now that she has
found him again, she can ask him, did you know why they were
laughing? and he answers, I think so, but with a shrug of his
shoulders he adds, insofar as there was anything to know. I'm
listening, says Antonia, now blind and deaf, lying in the coffin
that four men are lifting from the trestles and hoisting onto
their shoulders before walking to the doors out of the church,
followed by the priest still murmuring prayers as they pass
before Our Lady of the Rosary, she, too, blind and deaf
beneath the faded paint, while the congregation, now set free,
also sets off, with a sudden commotion of prie-dieux creaking
against the flagstones, and they form a long line behind the
coffin as it crosses the threshold and emerges into the blinding
light of summer. Next to the flower-laden hearse, Antonia's
godfather recites the last prayers, while drops of holy water fall
on the coffin like a stream of baptismal waters, before evapo-
rating in the heat.

Take her soul,

he says again, and he does not want to stop praying even
though he knows very well that he must soon join his family,
stop being the priest for a moment, and stand with them in a
row along the church wall, beneath the grimacing faces of

demons carved in the stone, to receive condolences one last time while the hearse will head out and take Antonia to the cemetery, where they will lay her in the family tomb in a place that was not planned for her, all alone, in the darkness,

Dread and trembling have laid hold on me,

he hears her moan,

In that awful day

whose coming can no longer possibly be put off,

When the heavens and the earth shall be moved,

and he turns away from Antonia, who is taken away from him while he thanks the singers and takes his place with his family along the church wall where he must yet again endure the presence of these people who have embraced him twenty times throughout the day but who are still shoving and jostling to embrace him again, sometimes saying their name, the village they come from, or their degree of kinship until they wonder, worriedly, do you recognize me? only feeling relief once he replies, yes, of course I recognize you, when in fact he is staggering under the constant onrush of condolences, his eyesight blurred by the burning sweat trickling down his eyelids, and obviously he doesn't recognize anyone anymore, not even the ones he watched grow up, Jean-Joseph C., Madeleine and Laetitia O., Xavier S., he robotically returns their kisses without even wondering who they are because he doesn't want to recognize anyone except Damienne T., who is suddenly there before him, unspeaking, she simply places her arms around his neck then disappears without even leaving him the time to thank her, yielding her place to yet another stranger, a damp and tearful man who, the moment he has done his duty, stands to one side to smoke a cigarette and laugh with friends. He hears laughter, and the laughter hurts, he cannot help it, what has become of me? he wonders, because in times past he liked to sense the persistence of life alongside the contemplation of grief, the carefree tactlessness of life, he liked the sound of jovial conversation up to the very threshold of the church, and he was never offended by the candor of laughter. Why is he incapable of finding it candid today? They will laugh, he thinks,

When Thou shalt come to judge the world by fire,

even on that day some of them will burst out laughing, an evil laugh where perhaps there is nothing to understand, but what does it matter, in the end, what does it matter, it's because of that laughter that I wanted to leave that country that changes its name too often, Dragan said, I couldn't stand it anymore, because it seemed like the entire country was suddenly shaking with the same laughter, a joyless, convulsive laughter, horribly contagious, and you heard it wherever you went, in the street, during meals with family, in the cubicles and offices of the administration where civil servants let you stew for hours while they laughed, and if they did eventually meet with you, it was to laugh in your face when you claimed you had a right to something, the way they laughed in the faces of the old women who came to ask for their pension, because every form of distress had become hilarious, they laughed, their faces contorted and frozen like masks while they split their sides laughing, and one day a recruiter from the Foreign Legion showed up in town to offer a remedy to those who suffered from the terrible fever that is war nostalgia, something it is practically impossible to cure because it is infinitely easier to go back to war than to leave it, and this guy was going around Serbia, he was a Serb himself, a guy from Niš, Dragan remembers him well, he didn't laugh when he met with them, Dragan and three of his friends who'd recently been demobilized, he invited them very politely to sit down then asked them if they had ever burned anyone alive, and as they all, somewhat surprised, said no, he asked them if they were prepared to do so, and after a moment's silence one of Dragan's friends said, if it means I can get out of here, I'll get started right away, preferably with a civil servant, and the guy from Niš laughed, but it was a good, hearty laugh, the way you laugh at a good joke, actually the question itself was a joke, a rather brutal and frankly dubious way of testing their motivation, but we were all motivated, Dragan said, so much so that I think my friend's response was completely serious, and three months later I was in France, with volunteers who'd come from all over the world, but above all Eastern Europe, Ukrainians, Poles, Romanians, other Serbs, and of course Croats, with whom he now had to run and crawl through the mud, but the physical hardship made him almost happy, and when he received his white *képi*, Dragan congratulated himself on having left behind a country he swore he'd never set foot in again, or in any case not as long as that intolerable laughter had its way with it, there were so many other countries he could go to now with the 2nd Foreign Parachute Regiment, strange faraway countries, in Africa, in the desert or the forest, by other shores where the waves would break in a burst of spray over a coral reef, I'd just have to wait a little longer and I'd find out where they were going to send me, Dragan says, now smoking a cigarette, a beer in his hand, his feet in the sand at the edge of a straw-hut café on the beach, where the waves are not breaking but lapping indolently in the stifling nocturnal heat. Lamp light illuminates his face as well as the hand holding the beer, and behind him the ocher walls of the citadel glow faintly. I'll take your picture one more time, Antonia says, and Dragan gives a vague wave of his hand, drawing on his cigarette. Antonia is not sure there is enough light, but she releases the shutter all the same, musing that for the first time in years she is making this gesture simply because she feels like it, and when her parents get the roll of film developed to send the photographs to the families of the wedding couple in Calvi, after the rings, the veils and cufflinks, the white lace, the guests at a banquet, and an exhausted couple running endlessly along the beach, they will come upon the portrait of a legionnaire whom they do not know and about whom they will never know anything. If Antonia could have seen the picture, perhaps she would have been satisfied, despite its technical imperfections. Only four spots of light emerge from the shadows: one side of Dragan's face, his fingers on the label of the beer bottle, the tiny incandescence of his cigarette, and, in the distance, the citadel suspended like a pale star above an invisible sea. Perhaps she would have concluded that she had finally managed to render the simplicity of the photographs that touched her so much when she was a child, the family portraits, the Polaroids, the ID photos tucked into yellowed envelopes or placed on tombstones, all of which, in their ruthless innocence, say the same thing, human beings have lived, but now death has come, in truth, death had already come, the moment an anonymous hand released the shutter in the Lubyanka building, in the prisons of Phnom Penh, or farther still, in an apartment in Santiago de Chile, where the sun backlit the face of a smiling student holding a leather camera case in her hand, a student who had no other tomb than this portrait, and perhaps then Antonia might have mused that all those prints she'd been so ashamed of— pétanque players, feast day committees, beauty pageants, or young men posing in balaclavas in the maquis beneath Moor's head flags, their rifles in their hands, all basically said the same thing, with the same innocence and, naturally, the same ruthlessness. On the stone sealing Antonia's grave, there is no photograph of her, even though her mother would have liked to put one there, which would have enabled her, when she came to sit at her grave every day, to see her daughter's face again as it had once been and not with its features distorted by a mother's false memory, but she looked everywhere and could not find one, either at home—other than old class photographs, the most recent of which was from 1982—or in Antonia's apartment, where she went the day after the funeral and found only, at the bottom of a cupboard, a shoe box full of old, undeveloped rolls of film, so that now she is weeping by a stone that is completely gray and almost bare, on which are only, carved in black letters, her daughter's name and the two dates of her birth and death. The air is still so hot that around the tomb, in the red light of the votive candles, the flowers on the wreaths and in the vases of stagnant water have begun to wilt. Antonia's godfather takes his sister's arm, come, he says, I'll take you home, and now that the funeral is behind her, she no longer has the strength to protest, and he leads her along the path through the cemetery, you have to get some rest, he says again, his tone full of concern, but he cannot help but think that deep down he is only trying to get rid of her so he can be alone with Antonia, he does not want to share his mourning with anyone, what has become of me? he wonders,

Lord, have mercy,

Christ, have mercy,

and he accompanies his sister to the room where his brother-in-law is already asleep, knocked out by sleeping tablets, and then he heads back to the cemetery alone, glad of his guilty joy, while the sun is setting into the sea. He opens the gate and walks past the vaults and the ancient black crosses tilting in the dry grass, a reminder that the forgotten dead are buried here, and he comes to an abrupt halt when he sees Marc-Aurèle sitting among the flowers, his head down, his hand pressed against the bare stone, and he cannot help but feel exasperated by his nephew's presence, the young man does not even hear him coming and eventually looks up at his uncle, his face so vulnerable and distraught that it is with infinite grat-itude that Antonia's godfather feels his heart opening at last to something besides his own sorrow, the grace, the burning coal, come, son, he says, going closer, and he holds his nephew pressed close, squeezing him as tight as he can, blinding him against his chest, holds him for a moment out of

AUTHOR'S AFTERWORD

It goes without saying that Antonia's photographs are imaginary, as is their creator, but the others, while their descriptions may be more or less accurate, are real photographs.

They are the work of Eddie Adams, Don McCullin, Gérard Malie, Kevin Carter, and Ron Haviv. The portraits described in chapter 7, apart from the one of Osip Mandelstam, can be found in Tomasz Kizny,'s book *La Grande Terreur en URSS,* published by Éditions Noir sur Blanc, 2013.

In the same chapter, the little girl in red was called Christina, and she posed for Mervyn O'Gorman on an English beach in 1913.

The name of the Chilean student referred to in chapter 12 was Sara de Lourdes Donoso Palacios. She disappeared in 1975. Her picture is in the Museum of Memory in Santiago, and her name is carved on a commemorative plaque at the Villa Grimaldi in that city.

Two photographers, or rather their fictional counterparts, play a vital role in this novel: Gaston Chérau, who reported on the Italo-Turkish war in Libya in 1911–12, and Rista Marjanović, whose work encompasses the first two thirds of the twentieth century. Without Pierre Schill, thanks to whom I discovered Gaston Chérau, and Zorana Vojnović, Marjanović's granddaughter, who gave me access to her grandfather's collection, this text would not exist. That shows how much I owe them.

I would also like to thank Jean Hatzfeld, Father Matthieu Rougé, and Jean-Marc Bodson, along with Milica, Melita, Borislav, and Nikola, all of whom enabled me to find my way through unknown territory.

In keeping with the promise I made, I cannot name the person whose help was most precious of all. But I know they know who they are, and that, after all, is all that matters.